Stolen Kisses from the Viscount

A Stolen Kisses Novella

Alanna Lucas

ISBN: 978-0-9985314-2-7

Sebastiani Press
P.O. Box 1234
Simi Valley, Ca 93062

Cover by Dar Albert

To my readers - Thank you!

Chapter One

"WE'RE RUINED!" PATIENCE cried into her trembling hands.

"We are not ruined," Patrick, Lord Leybourne, said as he gathered his sister into his arms. He detested that his family had been reduced to this. "I will think of something."

"You must marry with haste, before our situation is made known." Aunt Agnes worried the edge of the crinkled newspaper. "After Lord Howard's situation appeared in the Gazette, no young woman of fortune would have him." She tsked several times before continuing. "And he is such a pleasant fellow, what a shame." She raised her dull brown eyes to Patrick's. "You at least still have your looks."

"Despite your horrid reputation with the ladies, debutantes can not seem to resist you," his youngest sister, Parnell, chimed in.

"Really, Parnell, how do you know of such things? Certainly not from me." Aunt Agnes's face was red with embarrassment. "If your mother was still alive, she would die from shock. Patrick, do you hear what your sister is about?"

Patrick tried to hide the chuckle that was threatening to embarrass his aunt further. Agnes was the dearest woman in the world, if somewhat old-fashioned in her beliefs. She believed some things should not *ever* be mentioned.

Parnell wandered to where their aunt was sitting, and sat down beside her. She took Aunt Agnes's hand. "I am almost seventeen, Aunt Aggie."

"Age has nothing to do with it. You simply should not have knowledge of such things."

Patience raised her head off Patrick's shoulder and sniffled back the tears. "We should be discussing how to survive this, rather than discussing Patrick's rakish ways."

Patrick released Patience from his embrace and retorted, "I'll have you know I've never done anything that would bring any lasting disgrace to this family." Unlike their dead sire who'd had a penchant for betting at cockfights and other unsavory activities that unfortunately he'd been able to hide from them. "I. Am. Discreet." He emphasized each word to make his point. Patience drew her brows together and eyed him with a dubious look, almost as if she was unsure he was telling the truth.

He shook his head. Now was not the time to argue. Patrick knew he must marry to save his family from further ruin. Despite the steps he'd already taken to secure his family's future, the nagging in the back of his mind warned him that he was treading on unsteady ground. He couldn't even bring himself to tell his family about the bet with Pickering. They would be furious with him, regardless it was a sure bet and would ease their situation, biding them more time. He never thought he would be reduced to this humiliation. He had always gambled within his limitations and knew when to walk away. But he was willing to take this one last chance for his sisters and aunt.

Patience cupped her chin with one hand and tapped a single finger against her cheek as she delineated her plan. "I believe our first course of action is to make a list of debutantes with a large dowry."

"Why only the debutantes?" Parnell shifted in her seat, turning to address her sister. "If our situation is that dire, shouldn't Patrick try and woo every available female with a fortune?"

"Only the debutantes are not entirely aware of Patrick's past," Patience said with a wink.

"I thought it might come to this." Aunt Agnes reached for a sheet of paper that was on the side table and presented it to Patrick. "I gleaned quite a bit of information from Lady Blanch and constructed a list of eligible ladies with significant dowries."

"How much is significant?" Patience questioned.

"Fifteen thousand."

"That is quite a sum," Parnell gasped. "Are we really as bad off as all that?"

"Patrick sold off what he could and tried to save the rest. There is no money for either of you. We have barely enough to keep up appearances for the season."

His aunt and sisters conversed as if he were not present. Patrick wished he *wasn't* present for this. He would rather be exploring exotic pleasures in the crimson boudoir of the voluptuous actress, Yvette, than suffering this torture. Their words continued to chatter around him, reminding him their situation was indeed dire and needed his full attention.

Despite his efforts, all they were left with was this townhouse in London and an estate in need of repair in the country. Their staff in total consisted of three—a butler, a cook, and a maid. It was disgraceful. Patience and Parnell were the daughters, and now sisters, of a viscount and he was scrounging for money like some common street urchin all because his father had been a drunk and a gambler. Patrick would think of a way out of this predicament, his sisters would have their season, and everything would be fine.

He rubbed the back of his neck with force. "There must be a better—"

"If I could marry, dear boy, I would. But at eight and sixty I really do not have much to offer the opposite sex." His aunt's cheeks instantly reddened as the last word left her mouth in a mere whisper.

He knew his options were few— either accept ruin and disappoint his family, or give up his rakish ways and settle down with a woman he did not love. Resigning himself to the unfortunate task, he took the paper from his aunt and began to skim the list. "Lady Beatrice will not do. Her father watches her like a hawk."

Parnell stood behind him and looked down at the list in his hand. "What about Miss Oldfield? She is quite amiable."

There was one problem with Miss Oldfield though. Despite the fact she was ten years Patrick's junior, her countenance and manners suggested someone beyond her years—beyond Aunt Agnes's years even. If he *had* to marry, Patrick at least wanted some semblance of a content marriage.

"You may take Miss Juliana Baker off the list. She's recently engaged to Lord Neville, although I think she would have preferred a prince," Parnell said with a snicker.

Not wanting to be excluded, Patience joined in the discussion. "What about Miss Emson?"

"Who, dearest?" Aunt Agnes questioned.

Patrick was trying to put names and faces together when Patience clarified, "Miss Jane Emson. She is a few years older than me, but we became friends when we went to school together before Father..." Her words trailed off. No one ever spoke of what their father had done. Their combined thoughts alone probably had the bastard wrestling in his grave for peace. She cleared her throat before continuing, "Her father is a baron of little means."

"Then why are you even suggesting her name?" Aunt Agnes questioned.

With a know-it-all tone, Patience answered. "Lady Emson is the daughter of a merchant who did extremely well with his investments. Miss Emson's mother is providing her with a dowry of twenty thousand pounds."

"What's wrong with her?" Patrick huffed off out as his youngest sister enthusiastically cried, "She's perfect!"

"Nothing," Patience tsked. "She is quite lovely and very polite."

Patrick could tell by the tone in his sister's voice she was withholding something. An heiress in her second season must have *some* undesirable habit. He raised a questioning brow. "Patience?"

"Alright, she *is* a tad shy, but nothing a rake like you can't fix with a moonlit stroll or perhaps a clandestine affair."

"Patience!" Aunt Agnes breathed out in shock. "First Parnell and now you. Wherever do you girls learn such things?" She pulled out her fan and opened it with haste. Waving it frantically in front of her reddened face, she uttered, "I just don't know about you girls."

"Oh, Aunt Agnes, I am almost eighteen, and people do talk. Not to mention Patrick is hardly a saint." Patience uttered the later under her breath. Thankfully their aunt did not hear the comment. Patrick rolled his eyes—heaven help him.

Fumbling with the fan in her hand, Aunt Agnes scolded, "Even still, you should not say such things out loud."

"Aunt Agnes..." Patrick was about to come to Patience's defense but was silenced by the harsh glare his aunt cast his way. She was displeased with his influence over his younger sisters.

"Now, no more talk of...of such things. We best get back to the problem at hand." Aunt Agnes sat quietly for a couple of seconds before she began uttering her thoughts out loud. "I wonder who else might be suitable. There must be some young lady on this list that would do and..."

Patrick listened to his aunt with half an ear, too lost in their woes to think straight. He had exhausted every possibility, but he wasn't ready to accept defeat, or settle for anything less than an amiable match.

"*Patrick*." Both his sisters enunciated his name at the same time with great precision. He raised his head meeting their identical gaze. Patience and Parnell were exactly one year apart in age to the day. They looked like twins—a perfect blend of both their parents—in every way except for their eye color. Patience's eyes looked like the sea on a clear calm day, whereas Parnell's were a deep rich brown with flecks of gold.

Thoughts of his mother and father flashed through his mind. They'd had a love match. But everything changed when Mother died. Father had turned to the bottle *and* high-stakes gambling, a volatile combination he'd not been capable of winning against. Patrick never indulged in drinking. That was one limitation he was not willing to test. He was not going to ever become his father.

The heavy weight of their father's irresponsibility bore down on him like an anchor. If it weren't for these three women, he would have drowned under the pressure and gossip. It was one thing to be a rake and quite another to have his family be the subject of the latest *on dits*. Only with the aid of Lady Capers, the premier gossip in town and one of Aunt Agnes's dearest friends, had their situation gone unnoticed for so long.

Patrick was worried about how he was going to pull off such monumental feats as saving his family from ruin, rebuilding his reputation, and providing a dowry for his sisters. Unfortunately, he knew if he were to have any chance at success, he would have to give up a thoroughly enjoyable lifestyle—albeit one that had been neglected since his father's death. His name at present was only loosely associated with one actress. Despite all he would have to sacrifice, he would do anything for his aunt and sisters.

First things first, he needed to lure an heiress into marriage before the gossipmongers discovered their financial ruin. If their situation were to be revealed, his sisters would never be able to have their come-out. The gossips would tear them apart, right down to the last out-of-fashion secondhand thread.

"Patrick, are you listening?" Patience scolded. Unlike her name implied, she would not wait for an answer. "Clearly you believe Miss Emson is not sufficient."

Agreeing to marry to save his family was beginning to sound rather cold and callous, and this was coming from someone who had left a trail of broken hearts without much regard.

Patience crossed her arms as she huffed out a complaint. "Well, if she is not good enough, then I am at a loss."

He blinked several times, wondering what part of the discussion he had missed. "Who?" he began to question when out of the corner of his eye he saw Aunt Agnes slowly raise her head, a wide grin encompassing her face.

"I know who would be perfect," she said with excitement. "Her dowry is quite large. She must be nearing twenty which is a good age to marry." Aunt Agnes continued to ramble facts about the unnamed heiress who was to solve all their woes. "Poor thing lost both parents in a carriage accident several years back and has been living with her aunt and uncle—"

"Who is it?" Patience questioned before Patrick could even formulate the words through his rising impatience.

"Miss Aveline Redgrave."

∞∞

"I'm dying." Uncle Arnulf's words cracked the fragile lining of Aveline's heart.

The thought of losing someone she loved so dearly scared her. He was like a father to her and now she was going to lose him.

Forcing down the hard lump in her throat, she fought to maintain her composure without much success. Her voice cracked as she forced the words past her lips. "What do you mean? You're still young. You can't die."

He patted the seat beside him. Aveline trudged toward the sofa, dreading Uncle Arnulf's next words. "I am not facing my final demise tomorrow, but Dr. Watson has informed me that I should have my affairs in order. My heart has been troubling me a great deal as of late, and—"

"Wh...what are Aunt Winnie and I to do without you?" Her aunt sat perfectly still, her pale features devoid of all emotion. The pain in Aveline's heart was pressing against her chest like a sack of bricks. She felt as if her whole world was crashing down around her...again.

Uncle Arnulf inhaled deeply, and then let out a shaky uneven breath. "When the time comes, Winifred will go live with our son in the north." Before he even spoke the words, Aveline knew what he was going to say next. She had narrowly avoided that disaster four years ago. "And you will go live with Lord Redgrave."

"But I don't want to live with Father's brother." Aveline couldn't even force herself to use *that* uncle's name. Her father had been a saint compared to his brother's nefarious activities. "He is evil."

"Lord Redgrave is not as bad as all that, dearest." Aunt Winnie was the sweetest woman alive and Aveline adored her, but her greatest flaw was that she never saw the worst in people.

When Aveline's parents had died, it was only by the grace of God she'd not had to reside with her father's brother. He had been much too concerned with his new title and vast wealth to care about Aveline. Thankfully, Uncle Arnulf had encountered no difficulty in arranging Aveline's temporary guardianship. These past four years with her beloved aunt and uncle had been the happiest of her life.

"I still don't understand why—"

"Don't make this any more difficult than it needs to, Aveline. I tried to reason with Lord Redgrave, but he has issued his ultimatum, and you must accept." Uncle Arnulf's exhausted tone halted further protest. Aveline sat and waited for her death sentence to be issued. "You have two choices. You can either go live with your uncle or marry."

Aveline did not have to think for very long. Although she was not keen on marriage, it was the lesser of the two evils, and she would not cause her uncle further concern. "I will make my list this afternoon."

"List, dearest?"

Aveline knew her aunt would be appalled by her method of going about finding a husband, but she was not going to fall into the same trap her mother had been snared in. She was not going to charge in heart first and swoon at the sight of the first attractive gentleman who promised the world, and then turned his back the moment he had what he wanted. Her father had not even had the decency to wait until the ink had dried on the marriage certificate before he'd begun cheating on her mother. *Focus on the present*, she reminded herself. It wouldn't do Aveline any good to dwell on the past.

"A list of suitable gentlemen, Aunt Winnie."

"I think that's a wise decision." Aveline was caught off guard by her aunt's acquiescence.

"You do?"

Regret and sadness weighed heavy with Aunt Winnie's words. "I do not want you to make the same mistake my dearest sister made. She should never have agreed to your father's proposal." She exhaled on a long sigh. "But him being the dashing and extremely handsome gentleman that he was, she could not resist."

One thing Aveline was most certain of was that she would not have any trouble avoiding rakes and scoundrels. She had promised herself she would never marry or fall victim to a man like her father.

Since her parent's death, they rarely spoke of what happened. Even after four years, the shock of her mother killing her father and his mistress, then taking her own life was still too much to bear. Despite the rumors, the *ton* still believed that her parents had died in a carriage accident.

Aveline was almost too afraid to ask. "How long do I have before..." A raw grief overwhelmed her and choked her words.

"Lord Redgrave has generously agreed to give you three months." Aveline knew from the tone in her uncle's voice that he did not believe the timeframe to be at all generous. Lord Redgrave and generosity were not synonymous.

Panic like she'd never felt before ricocheted against her chest. Forcing the words past the hard lump in her throat she uttered, "I believe I will go and rest." Without waiting for acknowledgement from her aunt or uncle, she hastily left the room.

Once in the hall, she inhaled deeply and exhaled attempting to calm her nerves. She would survive this, just like she'd survived all the arguing and fighting, just like she'd survived her parents' death.

Walking through the halls she imprinted in her mind all the things she loved about this house. The tall ceilings and wide windows seemed to invite sunlight in even on the cloudiest of days, Delft vases in various sizes that were always overflowing with flowers— especially her favorite, red roses—and a white marble statue of a lion cub were among the treasured items. She would miss this house. Since living with her aunt and uncle, Aveline had felt like she was part of a loving family.

A coarse shiver ran through her settling into her chest. Tears she had fought to control streamed down her face, washing away the happiness she had found since living here.

Running toward her room, she ignored the servants who knew better than to say anything but were curious nonetheless. She stormed into her room, closing the door with more force than intended, leaned against it and slid to the cool floor. Bringing her knees to her chin she cried into her sea-green dress, the tears speckling the fabric like rain on a spring day.

She should consider herself quite fortunate to have delayed marrying thus far. During her first season, she had told her aunt and uncle it was too soon after her parent's death to even think of embarking on a new adventure. They had only been dead a year and the tragedy of their deaths had still been too raw in her mind.

Somehow, she had convinced them to give her more time in her second season. She remembered telling them she just wanted to enjoy herself. And she had. There had been no shortage of admirers, but common sense and a guarded heart had kept would-be suitors at bay. Now with her uncle's health in decline, she was faced with no other viable option. She must marry.

It was not as if she hadn't known Uncle Arnulf suffered from a weak heart, she'd just never realized the severity of the situation. Or perhaps she'd been in denial. He had always put on a good face for Aunt Winnie and her. The least she could do was the same.

She forced herself off the floor and lumbered to her writing desk, pulled quill and paper from the drawer and began to write down names of gentlemen and their qualities.

A couple of hours later, with sheaves of paper lay strewn across her bed, surrounding her in a tomb of names and forced decisions, she contemplated the list she had constructed. She wasn't in love with any of the men, but each gentleman met her criteria. None were gamblers or imbibed, there were no scandals attached

to their name—her family made up for that in spades—
and most importantly, none were rakes.

As satisfied as she could be under the
circumstances, she turned her attention to her
sketchbook. She only had three months to sketch all the
things she loved around her. Three months to sustain
her for the rest of her life.

Chapter Two

"IT WON'T BE too terrible." Aveline tried to convince herself as she stared into the mirror, adding the finishing touches to her hair.

She used to enjoy balls and soirées, but the luster from her second season had dulled. And now with Lord Redgrave's ultimatum, the thought of being out in society was even less appealing.

"You have no choice. Remember how much Uncle Arnulf and Aunt Winnie love you and have taken care of you. You need to do this for them." Ignoring any further fears, and with her words of encouragement to herself in place, she rose to retrieve her list of acceptable gentlemen. Aveline was hoping to narrow the list of a dozen dull men down to half this evening.

Returning to her dressing table and leaning both elbows on its dark wood surface, she cupped her face and stared at her reflection in the mirror once more. She had her mother's blue-grey eyes and her father's wavy blonde hair, but she did not feel like she belonged to either of them. A heavy sigh of regret coursed through her body. All she had ever wanted was her parents' love, but they had always been far too consumed with arguing to even notice when she was present. And now it was too late.

No sense in dwelling in the past, she reminded herself. She had a future to worry about. Picking up her favorite light blue silk reticule, she rose and trudged toward the drawing room, and what felt like her doom.

"Oh, Aveline, you look lovely this evening," Aunt Winnie exclaimed with giddy excitement. "I just know you will catch the eye of some handsome gentleman."

Aveline simply smiled at her aunt. She knew Aunt Winnie was attempting to lighten the situation and she loved her all the more for it.

"Your uncle is resting now, but looks forward to hearing all about the evening later. We mustn't tarry." Aunt Winnie headed for the door with such excitement one would have thought this was *her* first season. "This is going to be a splendid evening. Lady Trumble has always hosted magnificent events for each of her daughters, and tonight promises to be unparalleled with her youngest daughter having entered society."

Aveline did not believe her aunt came up for air during the carriage ride and her ramblings only continued while they waited to be announced. However, once inside, conversation became near on impossible as a combination of music, chatter, and gaiety penetrated the walls. The crush was quite extreme and Aveline could not help but wonder if anyone had actually declined Lady Trumble's invitation.

Hoping to retreat to a quiet corner, she turned away from the ballroom and came face to face with Mr. Fleming, a notorious fortune hunter if there ever was one. "May I have this dance, Miss Redgrave?"

Aveline could not very well refuse. She accepted his hand with reluctance. Despite Mr. Fleming's best efforts to engage her in conversation, Aveline focused on the dance, especially when he began to boast about his prospering country estate. She knew otherwise. Mr. Fleming's money woes had appeared in the Gazette two weeks previous.

No sooner had one dance ended and Aveline was returned to her aunt, then she was asked to dance by another. She knew her popularity was centered on two facts: her immense dowry and her uncle's ultimatum, which had already begun to make the gossip rounds. Despite the number of men who had tried to catch her fancy in the past, none had captured her heart. She was not going to marry a man who was only interested in her wealth. She would not make the same mistake her mother had made.

By the time the fourth set finished, she had endured enough. Claiming fatigue, she retreated to the refreshment room with her aunt. Fortunately, two seats along the perimeter—and a short distance from the main crush—were still available. She preferred to sit off to the side, it gave her the opportunity to view and watch those around her.

While her aunt was preoccupied noticing what every young lady was wearing, Aveline glanced about, further surveying her options.

Mr. Graunt, a rather large man with a horrid complexion and even worse teeth, was attempting to garner attention from any female who was within ten feet. Aveline shuddered. No, he would not do.

Lord Buxton's boisterous laugh ricocheted from across the room, drawing her attention. He was engaged in a lively conversation with Mr. Hughlot. She did not have to even think twice about Lord Buxton. He was a rake *and* a gambler, and far too similar to her late father.

Mr. Hughlot, on the other hand, was quite the gentleman: polite, well dressed, and an excellent dancer. There was no gossip or scandal surrounding his name. The only problem was he never had shown any interest in Aveline, or any other member of the fairer sex for that matter. Another name crossed off. One by one her list of eligible gentlemen was diminishing. With only three months to secure a proposal, time was of the essence.

Out of the corner of her eye, she spied Lord Leybourne, who sauntered into the room commanding attention with his Corinthian presence. *Look away. Focus on the gentlemen from your list.*

But her attention strayed back to Lord Leybourne. He was far too handsome and the only man who had ever turned her head. Ever since he'd asked her to dance in her first season, he had occupied her dreams far too often... *delicious dreams where he...* she shook the thought from her mind. He was a rake and precisely the sort of man she intended never to marry. She would *only* allow him to enter her dreams but never her heart.

Aunt Winnie kept her gaze straight but leaned slightly into Aveline and whispered, "Lord Leybourne is walking this way, dearest."

Aveline's heart stopped for a brief second before it began pounding wildly against her chest.

"Good evening, Lady Jagger, Miss Redgrave." He flashed a smile before turning his deep brown eyes on her. "May I have the next dance?"

Before her mind could protest Aveline stood and accepted his arm. Warmth instantly careened through her body, colliding with irritation. She was vexed with her eager response. She would have to try harder to maintain her composure and not fall victim to his irresistibly devastating smile and disarming dimples.

Lord Leybourne guided her through the crush, not brushing a single person. It seemed as if everyone parted to let him pass. She suspected his impressive height, broad shoulders and Adonis-like good looks contributed to his popularity.

"What diversions have you discovered this season, Miss Redgrave?"

"Nothing new, Lord Leybourne." *Remember he is a rake, don't let him affect you.* She gazed off into the distance and began her rehearsed speech. "It is always the same every year, dancing, routs, the theatre, and gossip." *Gossip*, she inwardly sighed. *Would it ever end?* The words poured from her mouth in an uncontrollable flow. "The gossip never ends until you're dead, and then it is passed on to the next generation. There is no peace. There is never any peace." Aveline blinked several times realizing how much she had just revealed of herself.

"I know what it feels like to be buried under the weight of the gossip."

"You do?"

"Yes." His eyes were filled with compassion and understanding. Something intimate charged between them.

The room around them disappeared when the first chords of the set began. They danced in silence following the required movements, but every time their eyes met, Aveline felt as if there was some secret communication only her body understood. His gaze was a soft caress that confused her mind and made her body tingle.

When the dance ended, Lord Leybourne held her gaze for several seconds. All thoughts centered on him alone. His deep brown eyes and lopsided smile made her insides do somersaults. She wanted to reach up and...

Oh, dear Lord.

"Shall I escort you back to your aunt?" His tone teased with another unspoken option, or perhaps it was just her imagination.

She nodded her head, afraid to speak for fear of revealing her inner thoughts.

Lord Leybourne escorted her back to her chaperone. Never taking his eyes from hers, he bowed elegantly as he said, "I enjoyed our dance. Till we meet again."

ഇൻ

Aveline was enjoying a peaceful morning after an exuberant, yet tedious, evening full of dancing, people watching, and narrowing her list. Resting her head against the plush sofa, she closed her aching eyes hoping to find relief, but instead was teased with images of Leybourne. One dance in the arms of a handsome rake and she was lost. His deep voice taunted her dreams *and* waking hours, promising untold pleasures.

"This just arrived for you, dearest." Aveline opened her eyes to see Aunt Winnie standing in front of her, with a letter in hand. It was best she pushed those other thoughts out the window.

She took the missive, recognizing the writing immediately. *The devil take him!* On a sigh, she opened the letter and scanned the contents. Any peace she had been experiencing was washed away on a tide of unwanted overtures.

"Well, what does it say?" Aunt Winnie's features became more animated. Clearly her aunt knew whom the letter was from. Aveline supposed she would not be able to hide the contents for long.

"It would appear Lord Elsworth is going to be in London and would like to pay us a call in a sennight."

Not satisfied with Aveline's summarization, Aunt Winnie took the letter from her hand. "Dearest, I think you have misunderstood Lord Elsworth's intentions altogether." Giddiness poured from Aunt Winnie's mouth, "He has requested a private audience with you. I believe he intends to propose. When he spoke with your uncle last—"

"He approached Uncle Arnulf? Why didn't you say anything?" Aveline's heart sank. As if her life wasn't complicated enough already. She did not want to be courted by the likes of Lord Elsworth. He was amiable enough, but she did not trust him. Elsworth was too much like his father, a scoundrel if there ever was one.

"I didn't believe he was in earnest. You know how fickle young men can be and besides..." Aunt Winnie went off on some tangent while Aveline festered in despair. Instead of three months to find a husband, she felt as if her time had been narrowed to a sennight. What was she to do?

"Dearest, are you listening?"

"I'm sorry Aunt Winnie, I suppose I'm still fatigued from last night."

"You will have time to rest for Lady Mayland's dinner party after we visit Lady Capers." Aunt Winnie glanced at the clock on the mantel. "We will leave in twenty minutes."

Thirty minutes later, Aveline found herself ensconced

in Lady Capers's orange and gold drawing room. White lace doilies graced every horizontal surface, the walls were crowded with paintings, and despite the warm day a fire had been lit. From the moment they entered, Lady Capers had not stopped chattering on about the weather, her aching limbs, and the latest gossip. The room and company were an assault on Aveline's senses. Although they had just arrived, she wondered how long they must stay.

"Miss Redgrave." Her name was called as if she had just got in trouble. "Have you set your cap on Mr. Fleming?"

"I do not intend to set my cap on anyone." Aveline's firm statement earned her gasps and wide questioning eyes from Lady Capers, who then gaped at Aunt Winnie with disapproval. Aveline quickly amended her statement for the sake of her aunt. "Not yet, at least. The season is still quite young." She tried to make her tone light and sweet.

"I believe that is wise." Her aunt relaxed with Lady Capers' approving comment. "And besides, Mr. Fleming would only bring you misery." Lady Capers continued on, delineating Aveline's next course of action. "You should marry a man of good breeding with his own fortune. That is the best way to ensure happiness. With your dowry, one would think you have the luxury of choosing for love because there are no financial restrictions. You can never be too cautious in this matter."

Aveline sat, wishing she were anywhere but here, enduring the lecture with quiet grace. The woman never seemed to take in air while talking and was the self-appointed authority on all topics of conversation. For the life of her, Aveline could not understand why her sweet aunt would keep company with the likes of Lady Capers, but for as long as she could remember, Aunt Winnie had.

A landscape painting on the far wall caught Aveline's eye, dulling the conversation around her to a low hum. The vast open countryside and cloud-spotted sky looked so peaceful. Aveline wished she were there right now, relaxing against the oak tree, reading a book instead of counting down the seconds until they could leave.

"...Speaking of good family, did you hear about Lord Leybourne?"

Just the mention of his name sent delicious shivers down Aveline's spine. Why did he have to be the one man in all of London who made her want to throw caution to the wind? He had haunted her dreams for a couple of years, but when he had taken her hand last night and led her to the dance floor, her world had tipped on its side.

Their dance had discomposed her more than she was willing to admit. She tried to push those thoughts further into the recess of her mind. He was a rake, she reminded herself for the umpteenth time. She was certain any gossip surrounding him must concern an actress, opera singer, or at the very least, a widow.

"No," Aunt Winnie gasped in anticipation.

"Well, after that unfortunate business with his father, the family retreated to the country and only just came out of mourning."

She had heard the many contradicting rumors but did not know what had happened. Aunt Winnie and Aveline leaned in with curious anticipation.

Lady Capers dragged out the silence, as was her wont whenever she wanted people's undivided attention or to reveal a piece of gossip.

"Don't keep us in suspense. Jacoba," Aunt Winnie pleaded. Aveline was quite taken aback by her aunt's tone and casual use of Lady Capers' given name.

Several more seconds passed before Lady Capers gave into Aunt Winnie's pleading. "One night, the old viscount was at Hell's Gaming House and lost a fortune." She shook her head several times before uttering, "It is really quite tragic. After his wife died he was never quite the same."

"What happened?" Aunt Winnie was practically on the edge of her seat.

"What happens to all good men…" Lady Capers leaned in and whispered, "they go mad." She leaned back in her seat with a sad sort of smile and placed her hand on her chest with much fanfare. "He was so distraught that he killed himself."

Aunt Winnie gasped behind her hand. "Oh no."

"And that is why Lord Leybourne detests gambling." At least that was one thing in Lord Leybourne's favor. Not that Aveline would ever consider him, he was still a rake after all.

"Has he recovered…what I mean to say…" Aunt Winnie fumbled with her words. She always loved to hear gossip, but was often embarrassed by her own eagerness. She had often said it was her greatest flaw. "Did he recover financially?"

"Yes. From what I hear, the estate is doing well and Lord Leybourne is now in the market for a wife to aid him with his sisters. He is quite devoted to his family." There was a gleam in her eyes and praise to her words that Aveline had never heard from Lady Capers before.

For reasons Aveline was unwilling to admit to herself, the information pleased her. Two things in his favor, plus Lord Leybourne was not in need of money.

Aunt Winnie shared her sentiments. "I'm glad to

hear it. Lady Leybourne had often spoken highly of her son. Poor thing. She was just too young."

But he was still a rake. Aveline forced herself to remember that very important detail yet again.

The remaining half hour was spent listening to Lady Capers delineating her plans for renovating the rest of her London home. They were informed with great enthusiasm that she wished every room could be as pleasant as the orange and gold drawing room.

"That was a most productive afternoon, wouldn't you say, dearest?" Aunt Winnie said as she ascended into the carriage.

Aveline was more confused than ever. Everything she had assumed about Lord Leybourne was not entirely accurate. There was a part of her that wanted to believe he was different and not quite the scoundrel she had thought him to be.

An image of her mother curled up on the floor beside an empty bottle of brandy, crying hysterically, heartbroken over Father's latest doxy, flashed through Aveline's mind.

No, she *would not* fall victim to Lord Leybourne's charms. She would keep her distance and remain levelheaded. It would be far too easy for her to succumb to the handsome viscount.

ℬℭ

When Patrick had accepted Lady Mayland's invitation to dine a fortnight ago, his plans for the future had lain in ruins. He'd had no idea who the other guests might be or how he could use the evening to his benefit. Much to his surprise and delight, Miss Redgrave had not only been invited, but as Lady Mayland informed him shortly after his arrival, he would be paired with the far too enticing beauty. Since their dance last night, thoughts of all other women had faded from his mind, which was a good thing since he was supposed to stay clear of gossip.

He walked about the room conversing with this lord and that about topics he could not even recall, as his mind was too distracted by the presence of Miss Redgrave. Although she appeared deep in conversation with Miss White, every so often he caught her glancing his way before she would quickly turn away again.

When dinner was called twenty minutes later, Patrick was still at a loss as to how to proceed. In the past he would offer suggestive smiles and sexual innuendos, but Miss Redgrave was a lady and his goal was marriage, not scandal. He had no idea how to win a lady over without seduction.

"Miss Redgrave," he bowed his head as he greeted

her. "We meet again. I believe we are paired together for dinner this evening."

Her mouth spread into a thin-lipped smile offering no encouragement for further conversation.

Never one to back down from a challenge, Patrick kept to the superficial conversation that was always deemed acceptable. "The weather has been pleasant."

"Yes, quite pleasant."

He was hoping to draw her into further conversation. "Have you seen anything of interest at the theatre this season?"

"No." Her answers were short, almost rude. A tense silence enveloped them.

Patrick decided to shift strategies. "You look quite lovely this evening." The light blue ribbon weaved intricately in Miss Redgrave's hair reminded him of his late mother. "My mother always wore a blue ribbon in her hair, it was her favorite color." Had he just spoken that out loud? Patrick never discussed his feelings for his late mother. Her sudden illness and untimely death were still too painful for him.

The heavy lashes that shadowed Miss Redgrave's crème colored cheeks flew up. There was an initial softness in her surprise that made his heart thump, but just as quickly it disappeared behind a cool façade.

Couples lined up and within moments they were

parading downstairs toward the dining room. The loud chatter from dozens of people echoed off the marble floor, offering no opportunity to converse.

Once ensconced in the dining room, the situation did not improve. Miss Redgrave sat silently, distracted by some unseen force. He wondered what she was thinking. Had he insulted her? Patrick was puzzled by her reaction.

To make matters worse, Miss Redgrave still seemed wary of him. He was sure she had heard the rumors surrounding his family *and* his reputation. If he was to stand any chance of winning her over, she needed to see him in a different light.

By the time the dessert course had been laid, he was no closer to enticing Miss Redgrave than before. If anything, it appeared he was rapidly spiraling downward into an abyss. He had never had such a difficult time charming a woman in his life.

Leaning toward her, Patrick whispered softly for Miss Redgrave's ears only. "You needn't be afraid of me. I am quite harmless."

"I am not afraid of you and although you might appear to be harmless, you are not a saint." She was the second female in so many days to state that minor character flaw, but her frank assumption of him lit a fire within. He suspected that beneath Miss Redgrave's composed façade and stormy blue eyes laid a fiery temptress.

Before he could tempt her further, Lady Mayland rose from her seat signaling the end of the meal. The other ladies in turn stood and followed their hostess.

Miss Redgrave did not say a word, but offered a small mischievous smile before she took her leave. Patrick didn't know exactly what it meant, but he was more than willing to find out.

By the time the men rejoined the ladies, Patrick was beyond anxious to have a moment with Miss Redgrave. His initial tactics during dinner had not worked, not until he'd teased her. Her response to his statement had intrigued him and he desired more.

"Lord Leybourne, won't you join our game?"

Patrick turned to the source of the question. *Lady Capers,* one of his late mother's dearest friends. Much to his dismay, the woman had taken it upon herself to watch over Patrick and his sisters.

"Perhaps another time." He offered no further explanation, and went in search of Miss Redgrave instead. He would not be joining any game, not tonight, not ever. Patrick had already crossed his invisible line with the bet he'd made earlier in the week with Pickering. He was not going to tempt fate further.

Across the room, he spotted Miss Redgrave sitting

alone on a settée, gazing off into the distance. She was a vision in light blue silk, an angel from his dreams.

"May I?"

She nodded her head in acquiescence.

He was not going to waste time on superficial conversation, best to get to the heart of the matter.

"I'm surprised you haven't yet married."

"I had no intentions of marrying," Miss Redgrave said in an adamant voice.

Most young ladies dreamed of marriage. Both of his sisters used to talk of little else. Then it struck him, she said she'd *had* no intentions. Finally, something was going his way. He wondered what had changed her mind.

"Why ever not?"

She shrugged her shoulder with a brief response. "I wasn't fond of the idea."

"But think of what you'll be missing." Patrick said in the sly seductive tone meant to entice that had never failed him before.

"I've been kissed before and I don't see what all the fuss is about."

"Then you haven't been kissed properly or rather.... improperly, Aveline."

Despite the nonchalant shrug of her shoulder, her eyes were wide with interest, and her cheeks blushed to a delectable soft pink.

Seducing willing actresses and widows was one thing, but an innocent was another matter entirely. But there was something about Miss Redgrave that didn't seem quite that innocent.

Patrick leaned in, closing the distance. "Challenge accepted."

A soft gasp left her lips as her head snapped forward. She offered a sideways glance. Her full pink lips were in a partial smile. "You are quite bold."

"Only when I want something."

Heat radiated between them. It had been years since Patrick was enticed by the possibilities of the chase. Aveline was no average lady of the *ton*.

Chapter Three

AFTER DEPARTING LADY Mayland's, Patrick was too restless to return home. In the past he would have sought out a pleasurable diversion, but since inheriting the title and a mountain of debt that amusement had become less appealing. He wandered toward his club, not sure what he hoped to discover but anything was better than roaming the streets in the middle of the night.

When he arrived at White's, he was mentally exhausted. The bet weighed heavy in his mind. He slumped down across from Pickering, one of his oldest friends and partner in debauchery since Eton. But for Patrick, that lifestyle had gone by the wayside with his father's death, whereas Pickering was still enjoying those nefarious entertainments.

Pickering held up a glass of brandy, the amber liquid danced in the glass from his unsteady hand. "Are you going to join me for a drink?"

"No." Patrick would not succumb to another of his father's vices. One was enough. The last time he'd tempted fate and imbibed was the day his mother had died. He had paid a heavy price for that ill-considered escape. He would not take that chance again. His sisters and aunt were depending on him to set things to rights.

"Are you ready to concede that you're not going to win the wager, Leybourne?"

"No, everything is proceeding as planned," he declared with feigned confidence. In all the years they had known each other, he had *never* lost at anything to Pickering, and he wasn't about to start.

"And you're still not going to reveal the young lady who has captured your heart?"

Patrick chuckled. "Falling in love was never part of the bet, only marriage." The problem was his heart was already softening. When he made this bet, he had not anticipated Aveline. But he had to see it through to the end.

"You don't need to be so touchy. I was just inquiring. I am looking forward to finally winning," Pickering said with a smug tone that made Patrick want to punch him. Pickering's ramblings were trying his last nerve. "I have need of your money. I still don't know how you managed to climb out of the hole the previous viscount had dug so nicely for you." The sarcasm practically dripped from those last words.

That was another taboo topic Patrick was unwilling to discuss. Only his immediate family and Lady Capers knew the extent of the Leybourne woes. And Patrick was not about to mention he didn't have enough funds to back this bet. *You've never lost to Pickering,* he reminded himself.

"Where there is a will, there is a way," Patrick offered casually.

"One day you are going to fall on your rump and I will be there, laughing in your face." Pickering lifted his glass and gulped the contents. "Yes, I believe I shall enjoy that very much," his words slurred out in a lazy drawl.

Patrick could not stomach this conversation any longer. He stood and stormed through the club with Pickering's laughter on his heels. His instincts told him he should have called off the bet, but he was not going to let Pickering get the better of him.

When he stepped outside, a cool wind and slanted rain slapped him in the face, urging him home. The weather had taken a turn for the worse. By the time he reached the house, he was drenched. But instead of retiring, he retreated to his cold study. There were hardly any furnishings left, just a desk and two chairs. The books that had once lined the walls had been sold, along with everything else of value. The only ornament left was an ornate wooden box he had made for his mother, but she had not lived long enough to see it.

Patrick went to the window and stared out into the darkness. If only he had known his father was gambling again, perhaps he could have stopped him. Rubbing a firm hand behind his neck he contemplated everything that had gone wrong over the past eighteen months.

Closing his eyes, he inhaled deeply. Too many things had been out of his control. He could not turn back time, but he could secure his family's future.

He *was* going to bring his family out of this. He *was* going to win that bet. He *was* going to marry Aveline.

෨൙

It had been a miserable night. The constant pitter-patter of rain on the window had kept Aveline awake all night. It seemed Mother Nature was just as impatient as she, as if they were both waiting for something to happen, but were content to be miserable until it did.

She could not forget the look on Lord Leybourne's face when he'd spoken of his mother. He'd seemed just as surprised as Aveline. She had witnessed a side to him that she never would've thought a rake like him would have possessed. Much to her dismay, that comment had softened her resolve against him. And hadn't Lady Capers said he would do anything for his family? *He is still a rake and rakes cannot be trusted.* Her argument was beginning to sound weak even to her own ears.

Aveline was trailing behind, her feet dragging, and her arms heavy with the weight of her small sketchbook. She hadn't really wanted to go for a walk this afternoon. If she were still a young child, she would have been kicking up dirt and pebbles in protest.

"Come along, dearest," Aunt Winnie called to her with an energy that bespoke someone half her age. Aunt Winnie had always been fond of long walks in the park and today was no exception.

It seemed as if everyone in London had ventured to Vauxhall after such an unpleasant night. Hordes of people were strolling along the Grand Walk. It was a fanciful parade of colorful bonnets and fashionable dresses, and Aveline was a willing voyeur. She enjoyed watching people rather than being on display.

"I do believe that's Lord Leybourne in the distance," her aunt commented. "I wonder who the young ladies are."

Aveline squinted against the bright sunlight as Lord Leybourne, flanked by two extremely attractive young women, came into focus. Even from this distance they looked to be identical. Aveline was all too familiar with the rumors that had circulated around her father, and assumed Leybourne enjoyed similar activities.

Uncontrollable jealousy brewed from within. Why should she care with whom he strolled with or what activities he indulged in? It was none of her business. And to think of all the hours of sleep she had lost dreaming of him gathering her into his arms and showering her with kisses.

She was still fuming when Leybourne and the two young women approached. "We meet again, Miss Redgrave." He flashed her one of his notorious debonair smiles, which only added to her angst. She would not be fooled by his suave mannerisms.

"Lord Leybourne, what a pleasant surprise it is to see you here this fine afternoon. I was just telling my niece it seemed as if all of London was out enjoying the day. The rain from last night has most certainly cleansed the air."

Aveline fought the urge to cross her arms and tap her foot. Last night he'd been so kind, even when she'd been trying her best to be aloof. But now he was parading his latest conquests in front of her.

"That is precisely why my sisters and I ventured to Vauxhall this afternoon." Leybourne flashed Aveline another one of *those* smiles, the scoundrel.

She glanced from Leybourne to one of his sisters, back to him, then to the other one. The resemblance was quite astonishing. The girls must be twins. Damn him for proving her wrong, and damn herself for thinking the worse of him.

"Lady Jagger, Miss Redgrave, allow me to introduce my sisters, Miss Leybourne and Miss Parnell."

"We are so pleased to make your acquaintance Miss Redgrave," Miss Parnell exclaimed with excitement.

"Yes, Patrick has spoken very highly of you. He said you are an excellent dancer."

"That's quite enough, Patience," Leybourne said with a lighthearted tease. An easy smile played at the corners of his mouth. "You might give Miss Redgrave the wrong idea about me."

Aveline watched the interaction between him and his sisters. She had always wanted a sibling and envied the affection that passed between them. He seemed to be such a caring brother. A pang in her heart struck to the very core. Leybourne's concerned gaze reached hers, his eyes softened with understanding. Perhaps she *had* been wrong about him all along.

Thankfully Aunt Winnie steered the conversation back toward a more superficial topic. "I hope we will see you this evening at Miss White's ball."

"I look forward to it." Leybourne stepped away from his sisters, turning his attention to Aveline. "Will you reserve me a dance this evening?"

"I would be delighted." Aveline's heart leapt for joy, but her mind scolded her for being far too eager. A few kind words and a sympathetic gaze did not erase Lord Leybourne's past. This was not what she needed if she were to stay firm in her resolve against rakes and scoundrels.

ℰ◌ℛ

When Patrick saw Aveline's reaction in Vauxhall earlier, he knew he would not have any trouble wooing her, and Miss White's ball was the perfect event at which to enact his plan.

This was going to be an easy undertaking. Kiss her thoroughly, seduce her, and then marry her. By his estimations, they would be married within the month. His financial woes would be at an end. Everything was going to turn out exactly as planned, perhaps even better.

The reeling in his stomach mocked and told him otherwise. Nothing in life was completed in three simple steps.

The moment Aveline entered the crowded ballroom, hushed whispers about Lord Redgrave's ultimatum danced through the halls.

Even from a distance, he was drawn to her. The elegant blue silk gown accentuated her womanly curves and brought out the color of her enticing eyes. Patrick edged through the crowd casually, wanting to be near her, but not wanting it to appear as if he was crossing the room to see her.

Sauntering over to Aveline and Lady Jagger, he kept his gaze focused on Aveline, demanding she look his way. But by the time he reached them, she had yet to offer even a slight glance in his direction.

He would not allow her nonchalance to interfere with his goal. "Good evening, Miss Redgrave." He bowed and then offered his hand. "I believe you promised me a dance."

"Lord Leybourne." Her features were reserved and composed. She nodded her head in acquiescence, and accepted his hand. "Despite what you said earlier in the day, I am quite surprised to find you here this evening."

Had she been gleaning information about him? The thought boosted his ego, but there was an underlying tone he was unsure about. "How so?"

She gave him a sideways glance. "There are no actresses or women of ill repute in attendance."

Clearly Miss Redgrave did not have any issue speaking her mind. Wanting to paint himself in a better light, he corrected her with an honesty that shocked even himself. "I am not interested in that sort of entertainment anymore. There are other things on my mind."

"Such as?"

Just then the music began. The dance did not allow for much conversation, but when they met on the next pass, Patrick whispered, "You."

Aveline's cheeks reddened and he knew it was not from the dance. They parted and changed partners. Several steps later, they rejoined, and he continued his enticement. "And kissing you."

Patrick was enjoying the effect he was having on her and decided to take full advantage of the situation.

When the dance came to an end, he did not return Aveline to Lady Jagger, who appeared completely enthralled in conversation with Lady Capers. Instead he changed directions, pulling her behind a boisterous crowd of nearly intoxicated young men, and down a candlelit hall. Within a matter of moments, he had pulled her inside some dark room and pressed against the door.

"So, you believe you're immune to my charms?" He whispered the words across her cheek to her ear.

"I know I am," Aveline said in a purring whisper that sent a jolt of excitement through his veins. He loved the thrill of the chase and nothing would give him—and her—more pleasure than for him to chase, catch, and seduce her.

He did not kiss her immediately. Instead he waited, brushing his lips across her jaw, breathing in her intoxicating scent. The tiny sounds mewing from her lips were like an aphrodisiac to his senses. She was caged between his arms. Removing one hand from the door he weaved a line down her neck, across her chest, circling one ample breast through the silk fabric. The rise and fall of her chest confirmed she was enjoying his ministrations as much as he enjoyed giving.

His tongue traced the soft fullness of her lips. He raised his mouth from hers and gazed into her passion filled eyes before claiming her mouth. The moment their lips touched, Patrick knew he was lost forever.

Aveline's hands explored his shoulders, settling into his hair. He fought for control as his mind reeled with thoughts of taking this simple seduction to the next level.

But the decision was made for him when Aveline pulled back. Her breathing matched his own labored breath, as she seemed to struggle for composure.

"Aveline, that was..."

"It was fine, nothing earth shattering." She muttered hastily. "Nothing I haven't experienced before. This was an...an interesting experiment, Lord Leybourne."

"One that I hope to repeat again."

Aveline ignored his riposte and uttered, "I best be returning to my aunt." She pushed off the door and away from Patrick's embrace. In a flurry of blue silk she left the room with haste.

Interesting indeed. Patrick knew he had Aveline right where he wanted her. He would enjoy stealing kisses from the sleeping temptress.

"Where have you been, dearest?"

The answer was far too complicated for Aveline to explain to her aunt, or really anyone for that matter. She had been kissed before, but those brief chaste kisses had been nothing compared to the flame Patrick ignited. Not for the first time, he had made her want to throw all caution to the wind and experience more. There was something in his kiss that made her believe she could have her own happily ever after.

Fortunately, the arrival of Lord Pickering distracted her aunt from further questioning Aveline's brief disappearance.

"Good evening, Lady Jagger. I understand Lord

Jagger is under the weather. I hope it is nothing serious."

"My husband is fairing much better. It is so kind of you to inquire after him." Aunt Winnie clearly had a different opinion of Lord Pickering than Aveline. There was something about him that Aveline simply did not care for, but could not quite name.

He bowed his head slightly. "Not at all. I was wondering if I might borrow your lovely niece for the next dance."

Aunt Winnie did not give Aveline the chance to answer for herself. "She would be delighted."

Without further word, Aveline found herself being escorted to the dancing hall. Nothing was like as it had been with Patrick. Thank heavens for that, or she would have suspected she was very ill indeed.

"I was hoping to see more of you this season, Miss Redgrave, or may I call you Aveline?"

"Miss Redgrave will do, thank you." There was only one man she wanted to hear her name from. She glanced past Lord Pickering and saw Patrick fuming off to one side. Part of her was thrilled. The other part desperately wanted to run into his arms and find some dark corner and beg for more kisses.

One dance after another and the evening was still no closer to being over. To make matters worse, Patrick was nowhere to be seen. It had been at least an hour since the last time she had spied him. Did he leave to find other entertainments? *Probably got bored, to tell the truth.*

Aveline was just about to give up when she saw him sneak outside onto the veranda. Her blood boiled. She just knew he was meeting someone else. She was such a fool to believe he might have deeper feelings for her. It was all a game to him, nothing but a game. Well, she was going to confront him and end this ruse once and for all.

Careful to avoid any prying gossipmongers, Aveline edged along the perimeter of the room and snuck out into the cool night air. The small veranda was unlit, cloaked in darkness. She blinked several times, trying to adjust her eyes when a large hand snaked around her waist and pulled her into a warm wall of masculine flesh.

"I was hoping you would search me out," Patrick said as he lowered his lips to her neck. With gentle movements, he edged her further into darkness.

"How do you know I wasn't looking for someone else?"

Patrick lifted his head. His eyes pierced hers with an unspoken desire that reached all the way down to her toes. His response came not in words, but in a trail of feathered kisses along her jaw. Her body instantly responded to the feel of his hands and the softness of his kiss. Warmth pooled in areas she had not known existed.

"Does that answer your question?"

She pulled out of his embrace. "I think you are far too confident in your abilities. *Good night*, Lord Leybourne."

She turned and retreated inside, but not before she heard him say, "Goodnight, sweet Aveline. Dream of me."

Heaven help her, this was going to be a long, sleepless night.

Chapter Four

AVELINE WALKED INTO her uncle's study with dread and anticipation. She did not want him to die. He had been like a father to her and she did not know what she would do without him. He was her voice of reason, the only person she ever turned to for advice.

"I was wondering when you would visit me," Uncle Arnulf said with a half smile. "You needn't be afraid, Aveline."

She approached him with caution. Aveline noticed the lines on his face appeared deeper, the circles under his eyes darker. He looked so tired and frail.

"I don't want to lose you."

"Aveline, come and sit." He waved her to the seat beside him. "This is something that is out of our control and instead of dwelling on what we cannot change, why don't we enjoy the time we have left together?"

Uncle Arnulf was right. She tried to hold back her emotions, but those pesky tears were threatening to destroy her resolve once again. He handed her a crisp white handkerchief. "No more tears."

Aveline knew she would never be able to keep that promise. "Thank you."

"Now, tell me what's troubling you."

"Why do you suspect something is troubling me?"

Uncle Arnulf narrowed his eyes and raised a questioning brow. "Might it have something to do with Lord Redgrave's ultimatum?"

Aveline nodded her head. "I don't know what to do. I seem to be the center of attention at every event, but how do I know if..." She stopped herself from saying Lord Leybourne's name. A couple of kisses were hardly an indication that he was interested in Aveline for more than just flirtation. It was better to simplify her problem. "You're a man. How—"

Her comment earned her a robust laugh. It was good to hear him laugh in such a way. "I'm glad you noticed."

"Uncle," Aveline giggled. "I am trying to ask for advice." Although Aveline adored her aunt, it was her uncle who she always went to when she had a problem. "How do I know if a gentleman is sincere in his advances?"

Uncle Arnulf leaned back and took in a long deep breath, his forehead crinkled in concentration. "Well," he exhaled, "when I was courting your aunt, I found ways to have moments alone with her, gave her her favorite flowers, and even wrote her poems."

"You write poetry?" Aveline could not contain the giggle bubbling up from within.

"I should've said that I attempted to write poetry. Thankfully, Winifred's decision to marry me was not influenced by my inability to write poems." He took Aveline's hand within his own. "My point is, I discovered what she enjoyed."

She inclined her head and offered a smile in thanks. She'd begun to edge off the sofa when her uncle stopped her.

"Aveline, there is something I would like to discuss with you."

She swiveled her body to face him. Anxiety knotted and twisted within her stomach.

"Although your aunt is quite enamored with Lord Elsworth, I will not force a union between the two of you."

Some of the weight that had been bearing down on her eased and the world seemed a little brighter with those words.

Aveline leaned over and kissed his gaunt cheek. "Thank you, Uncle."

ဆာ∞ભ

Under normal conditions, Aveline would have taken great joy in being at the theatre. She loved watching all the people, but tonight her thoughts were centered on one person. She had spent most of the afternoon thinking about what her uncle had said, and she was anxious to discover whether or not Patrick's affections were sincere. But how was she to achieve such a monumental feat?

Aunt Winnie stood abruptly distracting Aveline's musings. "Dearest, will you be joining me during the intermission?"

"I believe I will stay and watch the social butterflies flit about attempting to be seen." Aveline was in no mood to be social this evening. News of her dowry and uncle's ultimatum had spread like wildfire through the *ton*, and had gained even more momentum in the last few days, much to her dismay.

"We are *all* social creatures," her aunt said with a sweet smile. "Oh well, suit yourself. I will be right outside if you need me."

Aveline turned her attention from Aunt Winnie, back to those on the main floor. Apart from the mingling and conversation wafting through the vast space, there wasn't much in the form of entertainment. The crowd seemed rather sparse or rather she was uninterested in those in attendance. Her head was beginning to ache, and she wanted nothing more than to retire for the evening. Slipping into the shadows at the rear of the box, she settled in to the plush seat and closed her eyes.

"I was hoping to steal a moment alone with you." A deep alluring whisper tickled the back of her neck.

Slowly, seductively, his finger weaved an intricate trail from one ear, down the column of her neck, across her back, and up toward the other ear. Shivers of excitement careened through her body, her breath came in short spurts. She wanted nothing more than to turn around and succumb to his ministrations.

"Patrick," she breathed out.

"Shh." His whisper enticed her senses even more. She felt the exhilarating sensation of his lips against her neck. Her entire body was aflame with desire.

Aveline stretched her head back wanting to give him more access as he nibbled her ear and showered kisses across her cheek and lips before taking her mouth in a soft exploring kiss. A firm hand cupped her shoulder and glided over her chest.

An intense ache that needed release bubbled inside, and then just like that it was gone. Her body instantly felt the loss as hazy thoughts struggled to reenter reality.

Panic settled in as she realized what she had been

doing and with whom, not to mention in public where anyone might see.

Soft light from behind filtered into the space, followed by Aunt Winnie's giddy voice. "That would be wonderful. I'm sure Aveline would enjoy the outing."

Aveline whipped her head around looking for Patrick. To where had he disappeared? Had she just imagined the whole scene?

She brought her fingertips to her temple, hoping to avoid her aunt's gaze. Aveline looked down and on her lap was a single red rose.

ဢ၈

"Didn't think I would see you here this evening," Pickering said with a smug grin as Patrick entered the dining room at White's. Ever since he had given up his previous activities, Patrick had often felt like a lost soul wandering and unsure, and somehow, he always seemed to end up at his club.

"Habit of nature, I suppose." He crossed his arms and surveyed the surroundings. What was he doing here? He wanted to be in a dark theatre box stealing kisses from Aveline, tempting sweet sounds from her lush lips. *Control your thoughts.*

Pickering peered up at Patrick with a sly look that

did not sit well with him. "Have a seat."

Despite years of friendship, he didn't entirely trust Pickering. His friend had never played by the rules, and some nagging feeling told him not to turn his back on him. There was too much at stake to take the honest approach. With guarded caution he took the seat across from Pickering and waved a waiter over.

"Two more." Pickering pointed to the empty glass in front of him indicating his desired poison. Once the waiter was out of earshot, he probed, "How's the seduction progressing?"

Patrick detested *that* word. "As planned." His response was meant to be short, curt, and to deter Pickering from inquiring further.

Two glasses of brandy were delivered to the table. Pickering picked up the glass and stared down into the aromatic liquid before taking a sip. He relaxed into the seat and rubbed his jaw with his other hand. "I believe it's time for me to choose a wife." Pickering's statement seemed to come out of thin air, but his sly smile revealed something deeper.

"You don't say?"

Pickering had boasted for years that he would never marry. *What was he up to?* The hair on the back of Patrick's neck stood on end.

Swirling the amber liquid in his glass that he had

no intention of drinking, Patrick asked in a casual tone, "What made you change your mind?"

"Not what, but who, rather." Pickering took another sip of brandy before sating Patrick's curiosity. "Miss Redgrave," he said with a self-congratulatory expression that made Patrick's blood boil with rage. His oldest friend was about to meet an early demise.

With great restraint, Patrick managed to set his glass on the table instead of slamming it down and calling the blackguard out. He clenched his jaw tight until some of the anger dissipated. Crossing his arms, he leaned back and attempted nonchalance. "What made you decide on *her*?"

His comment earned him a harsh glare from Pickering, who stopped and peered over his half-empty glass. "I'm sure you have noticed her lush body and full bosom. I suspect she would be a most willing bed partner."

Patrick snapped forward and growled out, "You will not speak of Miss Redgrave, or any woman, in such a manner." Aveline Redgrave was his and his alone.

"Quite touchy this evening aren't you, Leybourne?" Pickering said with a lopsided grin.

"What do you want?" The room warmed several degrees. Patrick ran a finger along the ridge of his cravat, releasing his steaming fury.

"I am enjoying the wager and its effects on you." Pickering raised his glass then gulped half of the contents. "But I think the stakes are too low."

A surge of excitement coursed through Patrick's veins with the thought of winning more money from this blackguard. "What do you have in mind?"

"Clearly you are besotted with Miss Redgrave." Patrick met his harsh stare and was about to argue when Pickering added, "No use trying to deny it. I have known you for far too long." He downed the remainder of the brandy. "As I was saying, the stakes are too low."

"How much?"

"Ten thousand, plus the engagement must be announced by the end of the week."

Could he take this risk? In his mind, Aveline was already his. Securing an engagement and winning this wager would solve all his problems. *You've never lost to Pickering*, his inner voice taunted.

"Deal."

Pickering extended his hand to seal the deal. The moment their hands met, Patrick felt as if he had just made a deal with the devil himself.

What had he done?

He grabbed the glass and swirled the amber liquid, not bothering to look up.

"Are going to drink that or just stare at it?"

No matter what happened in his life, this was one temptation he *had* to resist. He placed the glass down on the table and pushed it toward Pickering. "Enjoy." Patrick stood and walked away before his anger got the better of him.

Chapter Five

PATRICK SHOULD'VE GONE straight to Aveline's uncle, asked for her hand in marriage, had the banns posted, then collected his ten thousand pounds. Instead he snuck into Lady Vance's soirée and was hiding in a dark curtained alcove like a common thief in the hope of stealing a moment with Aveline.

Music and laughter drifted through the air from down the hall. A melodious hum reached his ears. He peered out between the heavy curtain and the cool wall, spotting the object of his desire strolling his way. His patience was being rewarded.

When Aveline reached the opening, he pulled her into the dark recesses of the alcove and silenced her protests with a hungry ravenous kiss. She brought her arms around his neck and pressed her soft body to his. Heaven help him, he missed her.

"What are you doing here, Patrick?" Aveline questioned between kisses.

"I was curious about what diversions might be had this evening."

Misinterpreting his meaning, Aveline pushed away from him and crossed her arms. "You are at the wrong location if you are interested in *those* kinds of diversions."

Despite her stance, he could see the passion in her eyes and feel the desire emanate from her body. He closed the distance, enclosing her within his arms. "*You* are the only diversion I'm interested in Aveline."

"Oh." Her response was deliciously breathy.

Patrick brushed his lips against hers as he spoke. "Shall I prove it to you?"

She answered his question with an intense soul-searching kiss that had him begging for more. His fiery temptress had seduced him, mind, body, and soul.

Patrick deepened the kiss as he fondled one perfectly round breast through the fabric of her dress. Frustrated he could not feel more, he edged his hand under the fabric, and relished in the feel of her silky skin and hard nipple.

"Oh my," Aveline gasped.

Semblances of the real world slowly came into focus. *What the bloody hell was he doing?* If he stayed, Patrick did not know how long he could control himself. With great reluctance, he pulled back.

"I best be leaving you."

"Patrick?" The desire in her eyes was replaced with

confusion.

"I will not make love to you for the first time in an alcove." Her eyes brightened with excitement. He brushed a soft kiss against her plump lips. "Until the next time."

"There will be a next time?" She teased with a confidence that intrigued him.

"Does this answer your question?" Patrick's mouth swooped down to capture hers, and branded her as his own, leaving her in no doubt she belonged to him.

Resting his forehead against hers, he caressed her cheek. "Till tomorrow evening, my love."

With a final kiss, Patrick edged out from the alcove and snuck down the hall without encountering even one servant. Aveline's reputation was still intact. There was no doubt in his mind that after tomorrow evening, she would be his forever. Fate was smiling down on him.

₭₮

Keeping calm during the course of the day had proven to be most difficult. By the time the hour had come to ready for the evening's festivities, Aveline's insides were all knotted and only worsened as she entered Lady Guildford's ballroom.

Using the fluted white marble column for support, she stood on tiptoes peering over the elegant guests hoping to catch a glimpse of Patrick, but he was nowhere to be seen. It had only been twenty-four hours since she'd last seen him, but it felt like weeks. What if he'd changed his mind? What if she was mistaken about his affections?

Oh, her heart sighed, a man did not kiss like that if he did not feel some attraction. Her lips still tingled and her whole being warmed with desire as the remembrance of their last kiss danced across her heated flesh.

"Thinking inappropriate thoughts, Aveline?" Patrick whispered for her ears only in a deep seductive tone. Her name purred from his lips, further adding to the heat in her cheeks.

"I..." she swallowed hard, her throat suddenly dry.

"My thoughts are not far from yours." His deep brown eyes seemed to undress her on the spot.

She did not know what to say to him. Even if she tried to deny her thoughts, she suspected he would know she was lying. The problem was she did not want to deny what she was thinking *or* feeling. She wanted Patrick to show her more. She wanted to experience more of what her body craved.

He took her hand, guiding her toward the dance

floor. The first chords of a waltz resounded through the elegant hall. The soft glow of candlelight emanated from the large gilded framed mirrors. In his arms, she danced through the opulent ballroom on a cloud of desire. It was a magical moment where anything was possible, even falling in love with a rake.

They danced with melodic ease as if they were made for each other. She had dreamt of moments like this when she was a little girl, of a handsome prince who would rescue her and carry her off in the safety of his arms to some distant magical land, far away from her arguing parents and lonely existence.

Patrick squeezed her hand, bringing her out of her daydream. He tilted his head, nodding toward the pair of doors that opened onto the rear garden. Her pulse instantly quickened with the thought of having a moment alone with him. She looked into his smoldering eyes and smiled in earnest, not caring if she gave away too much of her own feelings.

Seconds later he waltzed her out of the crowded room and into the moonless evening. Thousands of stars twinkled against the dark of night. He tucked her hand in the crook of his arm and led her away from prying eyes.

Lanterns illuminated a wide pathway. Sweet, fragrant roses encircled them, guiding them farther down the path.

"This way," he whispered, guiding her from the main path to a deserted wisteria-lined trellis footpath.

She followed with excited anticipation, wanting nothing more than for Patrick to pull her into his embrace and kiss her as if she only existed for him. She longed for the warmth of his touch and the tenderness of his caress. Every time he kissed her, it was like she was being kissed for the very first time.

He pulled her into a dark arbor, encircling her within his strong sinewy arms, and moved his lips against hers devouring its softness. The kiss sent new spirals of desire through her. She pressed her body against his, tugging at his coat, wanting to feel more.

Patrick took a step back. "I didn't bring you here for a clandestine tryst."

Doubt reared its pesky head again. She lowered her gaze unable to look him in the eye. *He didn't want her after all.* Her heart sank into the pit of her stomach.

"I wanted…" He huffed out a labored breath. "That is…I'm in love with you."

Warmth radiated through her body as her heartbeat drummed against her chest. Those were the most glorious words she had ever heard. She jumped up, encircling her arms around his neck and kissed him firmly on the lips.

"I am so in love with you."

A wave of fear swept through her, carrying her joy out to sea. There was something she had to confess. Something she knew would haunt them otherwise.

Aveline had never told anyone of her upbringing or the fears that still troubled her since her parents' death. But when she was in Patrick's arms, she felt safe and protected. She knew she could share that part of her heart that had been locked for so long. She rested her head against his broad, firm chest. His beating heart soothed her troubled soul.

She did not look up at him, but nestled further into him. Tears threatened her resolve, but for once in her life she did not care if someone other than her aunt and uncle saw her cry.

"They didn't die in a carriage accident." She forced the words passed the hard lump in her throat. "My mother killed my father and his mistress, then took her own life."

She felt Patrick's heart beat faster and heard his sharp intake of breath, but he didn't pull away, quite the opposite. He gathered her closer and kissed the top of her head. She could not stop the tears from streaming inelegantly down her face. He didn't press her to talk, but continued to hold her, rubbing her back in soothing circles.

"I'm afraid," she whispered against his chest.

He caressed her cheek settling a gentle hand beneath her chin, raising it as he studied her features with concern. "What are you afraid of?"

This was the moment of truth. Their future happiness was at stake. Before they could go any further, she had to reveal her deepest fears. "That I will end up like my mother, full of hatred and anger. That my children will have an upbringing like mine, sad and lonely. That the man I marry only wants me for my dowry."

A long silence dragged out between them. She prayed he would not turn away from her in disgust. She chided herself for revealing too much of her inner turmoil.

The silence ate away at her heart. It was all too painful. She began to pull away, but he held her firm against him.

"As long as I have breath in my body you have nothing to fear."

His words warmed her, filling every crevice of her fragile heart. She reached up and brushed a kiss across his lips. His response was slow and thoughtful, surprisingly gentle. He kissed away all the fear and doubt that had been consuming her for most of her life until all that was left was a rising passion.

He pulled back, cupping her face within his large masculine hands. The warmth of his smile echoed in his voice. "I think we best return before your aunt notices how long you've been gone."

ଔଓ

What began as a plan to marry in order to save his family from ruin had turned into so much more. Somewhere along the way he'd fallen in love with Aveline. He adored her kind heart, her sweet yet seductive smile, and the way she made him feel. When he was near her, he wanted to be a better man. He wanted to protect her, take away her fears, to make her laugh, and to share his life with her.

He stormed through the dimly lit streets with only one destination in mind. It was essential he spoke with Pickering tonight. He was going to set everything to rights. He had to. He'd meant every word he spoke to Aveline. Once the bet was dissolved, he would go to her uncle and explain his situation.

By the time he reached his club he was in a foul mood, and it only worsened when he discovered Pickering had already been and gone, and was on his way to Hell's Gaming House.

Patrick clenched his teeth as he made his way to

the infamous gambling haunt. Of all the bloody places Pickering could go, it had to be the same one where his father had gambled on the night of his death.

When he reached Hell's Gaming House, he was in no mood for conversation, pleasant or otherwise. He detested gambling halls and this one more than all the others combined. The moment he walked into the opulent setting, his stomach churned with disgust.

Flashbacks of his father returning home drunk and sobbing through apologies coursed through his mind. The viscount had promised Patrick that he would set everything to rights, but instead the fool took his own life leaving Patrick to clean up his disastrous affairs. Perhaps one day Patrick might be able to reconcile with the ghosts of his past and remember his father as the caring and loving man he had been when his wife had been alive. But for now, Father was the bastard who threatened all Patrick held dear.

"What are you doing here?" Pickering snickered up at Patrick, his cards fanned in one hand. "I thought you considered yourself above this sort of activity."

"I am here on official business." Why had he ever kept such company? Glaring down at Pickering he said, "I would like a private word with you."

Patrick strolled away, knowing Pickering would follow. He always did.

The private parlor was not private enough for Patrick. Even walls had ears and he was not going to leave anything to chance. Gossipmongers were not restricted to only the female population.

Pushing past arriving patrons, he made his way outside into the cool night air. It was hard to believe less than an hour ago he was enjoying Aveline's company, and now he was dealing with this bastard. At that moment he detested himself for making the bet, and Pickering even more for goading him into it. This was one mistake he would rectify and would not repeat ever again.

"What's this all about?" Pickering huffed out with a wheeze, his slightly rotund belly rising and falling rapidly as he attempted to catch his breath.

"I'm calling off the bet." His muscles and fists tightened in readiness, prepared for a fight. "I want it removed from the books. I don't care how, I just want it done."

Patrick's demand earned him a gruff huff as Pickering struggled to understand. "What? I thought…"

He stepped in closer, towering over Pickering. His stance was meant to be threatening. Patrick narrowed his gaze challenging Pickering to argue. "It is not up for discussion, not with me, not with anyone."

Pickering stumbled through his words. "Of course,

I...I would never—"

"Make sure you don't." Patrick turned and walked away, but not before catching an odd gleam in Pickering's eyes. He hoped it was only his imagination otherwise he might have to do bodily harm to one of his oldest friends.

With that out of the way, Patrick could focus on the next step. He needed to determine the best way to approach Aveline's uncle. He had nothing to offer but his heart. Patrick hoped it was enough.

Chapter Six

IT HAD BEEN a long time since Aveline had slept through the night not haunted by nightmares. But the peace she had only recently discovered was abolished by the arrival of Lord Elsworth.

"My dear," Lord Elsworth said as he swooped into the room like a hawk. "It has been far too long since I have enjoyed your company."

Aveline forced a smile while her insides churned with revulsion. "Good afternoon, Lord Elsworth. I trust your journey was pleasant and uneventful."

"Only one mishap, but completely worth the trouble in order to see you." He flashed her a smile she supposed was meant to make her weak at the knees, but there was only one man who had that effect on her.

"My aunt will be sorry to have missed your visit, she is with a friend this afternoon," Aveline rambled out, uncomfortable with Lord Elsworth's presence.

"Actually, I am glad to have a moment alone with you." He stepped in closer. His off-putting scent of sandalwood and stale liquor was overbearing. "There is a pressing question and I simply cannot contain my ardor for you any longer."

Aveline was not one to string a man along. Desperate to discourage him, she started to explain the situation. "Before you continue, I must inform you Lord Elsworth that my affections are engaged elsewhere." As the words began, her confidence rose.

"Engaged elsewhere?" He stared at her, baffled and confused.

"Yes."

"Did you not receive my letter? I thought we had an understanding."

With hands on her hips, Aveline confronted him. "And what understanding might that have been? You presume because our fathers were friends that gave you some right—"

"Miss Redgrave, I am quite appalled by this turn of events."

"You are mistaken Lord Elsworth, I am the one who should be appalled. There has never been an understanding."

He raised his brow and with a hard smile that suggested he held the upper hand said, "Lord Jagger might say otherwise."

"My uncle supports my decision."

Lord Elsworth's face paled with the lie he'd just

been caught weaving.

"I believe it is best that you take your leave, Lord Elsworth."

Despite the calm exterior Aveline fought to maintain, her insides were quivering with strength she had not suspected herself capable of having.

Thankfully she did not have to ask him twice. Lord Elsworth grabbed his hat and with much haste stormed to the door without another word.

Aveline slumped on to the sofa relieved that was over with. It seemed as if only five minutes had passed when another guest—and not the one whom Aveline had been hoping for—was announced.

"Lord Pickering is here to see you, Miss Redgrave."

She rolled her eyes heavenward, stood and smoothed the front of her dress with shaky hands. Aveline was in no mood to keep such company. Lord Pickering rushed into the room, his brows drawn together in a grave expression.

"I wish I could say good afternoon, Miss Redgrave, but I have come on unpleasant business."

Aveline hardly knew the man, but was taken aback by Lord Pickering's lack of social graces. What sort of man charged into a room announcing unpleasantries to a mere acquaintance?

Before she could form any words, he began to

apologize, "I do hate to be the bearer of bad news, but I would rather you know the truth than to suffer at the hands of gossips."

It was a rather bold statement that left Aveline even more confused.

"It would appear you are the subject of quite a scandalous wager."

"Me? I...I don't understand." Aveline had a sinking feeling she did, in fact, understand. *Patrick.* She had opened her heart and revealed her fears to a man no better than her father. Everything she'd believed had been a lie. Every instinct she had ignored was now screaming, *I told you so!*

"Certainly, you are familiar with the betting books at White's?" Aveline nodded. Her first suspicion was confirmed. With a light gesture of her hand, she encouraged Pickering to continue. "Several weeks ago, Leybourne was boasting about his plan to marry a lady of great fortune in order to settle his debts. Although the young lady's name was omitted from the books, based on recent, shall we say speculation, your name has been connected with the bet."

Attempting to keep all emotion from her face, Aveline sat down on the sofa and remained motionless.

"What do you mean speculation?"

"It is rumored that you and Leybourne are having a

clandestine affair."

"But how?" All the loneliness and despair she had felt as a young girl crept back up and threatened to swallow her whole.

"How do any of these things begin?" Pickering sat down on the sofa beside Aveline. Although he did not touch her, she suspected he wanted to, based on his close proximity. The thought made her shudder. "Oh, I've upset you." He edged closer another inch. "I will personally squash any further rumors, Miss Redgrave. You have my solemn promise."

Not knowing what to say, she mumbled, "Thank you." Horrid thoughts raced through her hazy mind. She brought her hand to her aching head. "I...I don't mean to be rude, but I would like to be alone."

"Of course, my dear. I will take my leave." Pickering grabbed her other hand. "Please know that I will do everything within my power to see that your reputation does not suffer."

Aveline could not find the energy to respond. Closing her eyes, she turned her head away hoping the feeling that she was trapped in a nightmare would go away.

She heard Pickering say his goodbye, but did not look his way. Only when she heard the door close did she open her eyes and force her thoughts to the present. Somewhat dazed and confused, she stood and wandered restlessly around the room trying to make sense of it all.

Fifteen minutes later, the source of her angst was announced.

"Miss Redgrave, Lord Leybourne is here to see you."

Aveline wanted to scream. This was quickly becoming the worst day of her life.

Despite the pleasant day outside, the air chilled the moment Patrick was shown into the drawing room. Aveline looked beautiful in a blue and white striped dress, but when she turned her cool blue-grey eyes on him, he knew instantly she had heard the gossip. His heart lurched with a mixture of guilt and despair.

"Aveline—"

"Do not use my given name, you lost that privilege the moment you placed that bet." She retorted in cold sarcasm.

Patrick was not about to mention all the times he did use her given name after he had made the bet, or the intimacies they had shared. He was here to apologize.

"Very well, Miss Redgrave, allow me to explain—"

"No." She stood with her arms crossed. Her tone

was firm, final. "You lost that privilege as well."

Patrick stood in utter bewilderment, wondering what topic of conversation he *was* allowed. How was he supposed to apologize or even explain why he'd made the stupid bet if she would not allow him to speak?

The silence dragged on between them until Aveline erupted like a volcano.

"How dare you! I confided in you, told you my deepest fears and you offered sweet words and passionate kisses when all the while you were using me for my dowry."

"It may have started out that way but..."

"So you admit it?"

Patrick was not going to lie. Aveline deserved the truth. "Yes."

"Did you ever tell me the truth?" Aveline stood her ground, which he would have admired immensely if the situation were different.

"I did not lie about my affections, or how my father ruined us, or anything else." She remained still. Her features were emotionless. Patrick ran a trembling hand through his hair. "Damn it, Aveline, I love you."

Her head snapped up. Fear, anger, and passion flashed across Aveline's features. With shoulders squared, she sucked in a deep breath. "Goodbye, Lord Leybourne."

She practically ran from the room, leaving him with a raw grief that gnawed away at his soul. *What had he done?*

೮ාೞ

Four days had passed and Aveline still would not speak to Patrick, would not see him, or acknowledge any of the gifts he had sent her.

He was at a loss over what to do. He knew he was wrong, but Aveline would not even let him attempt to apologize or make amends.

Patrick paced the length of the cold, sparsely furnished chamber. The guilt that had been reeling within since this fiasco had begun was slowly killing him. He could not sleep. He could barely eat. Not to mention that his sisters and aunt were making his life a living hell.

The only satisfaction he had experienced of late was when he'd confronted Pickering. The bastard had tried to deny his involvement in spreading the lies, and only confessed when Patrick threatened to call him out. Pickering was a horrible shot and knew Patrick would not miss his target at any cost. Instead, Pickering retreated to the country nursing a black eye and a broken nose.

Having solved one problem, Patrick had turned all his efforts to winning back Aveline. How could he make her understand why he was so desperate to save his family?

He stopped and stared into the empty fireplace. What could he...*that's it*. Patrick flung open the door and hurried through the dark to his study. He lit a couple of candles, then rifled through the drawers of his desk. He pulled out several sheaves of paper, and got to work.

This was his last hope.

Chapter Seven

AVELINE WAS TIRED of visitors—friends wondering why she refused to attend social gatherings, and casual acquaintances wanting to know exactly what happened. But Lady Capers was by far the worst visitor she'd had dealt with over the past several days. She had been relentless in her questioning and insisted on giving her opinion on how Aveline should handle the situation, almost begging her to give Lord Leybourne another chance. Even Aunt Winnie had tired of her friend, asking Lady Capers to leave in a firm, yet polite sweet tone.

Aveline was certain she had received at least a dozen visitors thus far. She was exhausted. Poor Aunt Winnie was exhausted too and would probably be abed for days with a headache. At least her aunt had been able to retire upstairs after the last inquisitive caller departed. Unfortunately, just when Aveline thought her day was at an end, two more guests were announced.

"Miss Leybourne and Miss Parnell are here to see you, Miss Redgrave."

She sucked in her breath and steeled her nerves for what was sure to be a difficult visit.

The almost identical sisters rushed into the room. Miss Leybourne went straight to Aveline and embraced her. "How are you?"

"Patience, let Miss Redgrave breath."

Aveline eased out of Miss Leybourne's embrace, took her hand and guided her to the sofa. "Come, let's sit."

Despite her anger and hurt over what Lord Leybourne had done, she was not going to be rude to his sisters. It was not their fault their brother was a pompous ass.

Miss Parnell took the seat across from her sister and Aveline. "You mustn't think so ill of our brother," Miss Parnell said in a most sincere tone that Aveline did not doubt. "He was just trying to protect us and Aunt Agnes. When Father..." she cleared her throat as if brushing over unpleasantries.

Aveline was all too familiar with that motion. It was one she had perfected anytime anyone asked her something she did not want to answer, especially regarding her parents.

Miss Parnell sighed, "When Father died, he left the estate in ruins. Patrick tried all sorts of things, but—"

Miss Leybourne jumped in and finished where her

sister left off. "He was unable. All he managed to do was pay off Father's debts, but there is nothing left. He did it to save us."

Lord Leybourne's sisters clearly thought very highly of him, but Aveline was not going to be made to feel guilty. "He deceived me and used me for his own advances."

"Our brother *can* be selfish." Miss Leybourne paused and gazed into the distance as if recalling a distant memory. "No, he used to be quite selfish and self-centered."

"But since Papa died, he *has* changed," Miss Parnell chimed in. "And since he met and began courting you, he has been nothing but determined to win you over. Please say you will give him another chance."

Miss Parnell's gaze shifted. "Where did you get that?" She pointed to the small ornate box on the side table. Despite the sender, Aveline could not dispose of the intricate blue and gold Florentine tole trinket box. Someone had lovingly toiled over the beautiful pattern.

With hesitance Aveline answered. "Lord Leybourne sent it to me."

A soft gasp exited Miss Parnell's lips. "Oh my."

Aveline glanced back and forth between the sisters. "What?"

Surprise laced Miss Leybourne's voice. "Patrick made it for Mother shortly before she died. Despite its value, he refused to sell it."

Aveline was speechless. He had sent one of his most valuable possessions to her? He sent her something he had made for his mother? Her mind scrambled for answers. The anger that had been consuming her for days gave way to disbelief. Why would he do this?

"Whatever is the matter?" Miss Leybourne said as she clasped Aveline's cold hand in hers.

Aveline's world tilted on its side and began to spin. She blinked rapidly trying to focus on her guests, but all she could think about was Lord Leybourne. The fragile wall she had built around her heart had begun to crumble. She knew what his mother had meant to him.

"Nothing." She swallowed the truth. "I believe it's time for me to ready for this evening."

"Of course, Miss Redgrave," Miss Parnell said as she stood, nodding her head for her sister to follow.

Miss Leybourne did not release Aveline's hand as she stood. She looked deep into Aveline's eyes and without flinching said, "I believe he truly loves you. Try and forgive him. These last few years have not been easy on him."

Lord Leybourne's sisters departed, leaving Aveline

more confused than ever. She stood for countless minutes, her arms wrapped about herself trying to find comfort. She worried at her bottom lip until it ached.

Time stood still as events from the past couple of weeks played over and over in her mind. Anxiety, despair, and other unnamable emotions coursed through her body only adding to her confusion.

Strolling to the side table, she picked up the beautiful Florentine box. The pattern was simple, yet so elegant. She imagined Patrick toiling away at the intricate details, wanting to make it perfect for the woman who had held a special place in his heart. Sadness crept into her heart. He loved his family and they loved him in return.

"Miss Redgrave." Dunn entered the room for what felt like the hundredth time that day to announce yet another visitor. She looked up to the ceiling wondering who else wanted to hear what happened first hand, offer advice, or scold her for being too much like her late mother. Aveline wanted to break down and cry, or scream until she went hoarse. "Lady Leybourne has respectfully asked to have an audience with you."

Aveline did not have to wait long before an elderly woman with a forlorn face trudged into the room. "Miss Redgrave, I'm Lady Leybourne, Patrick's aunt." She held her thin bony hand up to halt Aveline from speaking. "Please." Her voice quavered with emotion as she spoke. "It has taking me several days to muster the courage to speak to you."

"Please have a seat." Aveline waved her toward the sofa then sat down beside her.

No sooner had she sat down, Lady Leybourne blurted out, "It's all my doing."

Aveline sat quietly and listened to his aunt's confession with bewilderment.

"I am the one who made the list. I am the one who suggested your name."

"But he was the one who made the wager." She argued against Lady Leybourne's confession.

"To save us." Lady Leybourne grabbed both of Aveline's hand and held them firmly within her own. The gesture took her aback, she was not used to such affection. "Do you know what Patrick did after he left Lady Guildford's ball that night?"

Aveline shook her head in slow measures, wondering what Lady Leybourne could possibly say that would change her heart.

"Patrick meet with... with that no good...Pickering and called off the bet." Lady Leybourne seemed flustered and embarrassed by her words.

"P...Pickering?"

Lady Leybourne's brows creased together. "Are

you acquainted with him?"

Her breath came in heavy gulps. "It was Pickering who delivered the news of the wager." Aveline leapt off the sofa, fighting to control her anger. "He said nothing about the bet being called off. The blackguard lied to me, made me believe Patrick did not care."

Aveline's rant had discomposed Patrick's aunt who was red all over. The older woman was so similar to Aunt Winnie. "I'm sorry. I should not have spoken in such a manner."

Lady Leybourne stood and smiled thoughtfully. "Do not worry, Miss Redgrave." She stepped away to take her leave before turning back toward Aveline. "Will you promise you'll at least think about why Patrick felt he had to do what he did?"

"I promise." It was a vow she would not have any trouble keeping.

After Lady Leybourne left, Aveline decided it was time to retreat to the confines of the upper floors, far away from any other possible visitors. After all that had occurred during the course of the day—the droves of callers, and the multitude of revelations and gossip— this was how she was to end her day, in hiding. She didn't know if she could handle any more confessions in one day.

She had no intentions of going out this evening, but decided it was too early to sequester herself in her room. With the constant arrivals, Aveline had not had the opportunity to visit her uncle. Earlier in the day, Aunt Winnie had informed her that Uncle Arnulf was feeling better and Aveline was anxious to see for herself.

Standing outside his study, she took a brief moment to gather her senses and conceal her emotions. She was not going to wear her heart on her sleeve. Taking in a deep breath, she stood tall and strolled into Uncle Arnulf's study with none of the confidence she was trying to portray.

The sight of Uncle Arnulf sitting behind his desk halted her steps. No longer were his features sallow and gaunt, but a healthy glow. His eyes shone bright with life and purpose.

"You look wonderful, Uncle." Tears of joy trembled on her eyelids. She hurried over to him and encircled her arms around his neck. He patted her back with a gentle motion.

Uncontrollable tears streamed down her face, absorbed by his coquelicot banyan.

"Now, now, Aveline. It's going to be all right. I'm doing much better." He pulled back, searching her eyes. "What has happened to cause you such distress?"

Aveline was not going to burden Uncle Arnulf with all that had happened. She pulled a chair beside his and sat next to him. "Everything is fine. I believe I am just a little fatigued from all the visitors this afternoon."

Her uncle adjusted himself, turning to face her. "I had a most interesting visitor this afternoon as well."

"Oh?" She had been confined to the drawing room all day, is that why she hadn't noticed who'd come to call on her uncle?

"Perhaps you know him?"

Aveline was unsure where the direction of this conversation was going, but deep down she was not sure she liked it.

"Lord Leybourne."

Those two words shook her world sending the frayed pieces of her emotions into a whirlwind. "Why did..." She swallowed her question with hopeful anticipation as to why Patrick had requested an audience with her uncle.

"He asked for a loan."

"A loan?" Not exactly the romantic idea that first came to mind.

"Lord Leybourne has some excellent ideas on how to turn around his country estate, but needs funds in order to do so." She listened to her uncle, torn by conflicting emotions. "He is quite an intelligent chap."

Aveline tried to hide her annoyance, but to no avail. "Is that *all* the two of you discussed?"

Uncle Arnulf chuckled, sending a blush of embarrassment to Aveline's cheeks. "We also discussed you, dearest."

She felt a little lightheaded. There were just too many emotions consuming Aveline. She did not know whether to laugh or cry.

"Lord Leybourne has made his intentions known. He does not want your dowry. Only once he turns things around and pays back the loan will he court you."

"That is his stipulation?"

"Yes. He even drew up a formal agreement."

Uncle Arnulf handed Aveline the paper. She scanned the contents, hardly believing what she was seeing. "This could take him years to pay back. What of Lord Redgrave's ultimatum?" Her voice rose with each word she spoke.

Uncle Arnulf leaned in and whispered, "The choice is yours, Aveline."

Without a doubt, the choice was clear in her mind.

"Thank you, Uncle Arnulf." She kissed his cheek before running from the room. Tonight was the night she would seize her happiness with both hands and never let go.

ဧဢ

After an eventful day full of callers, Aunt Winnie had declared herself in no condition to emerge from her chamber and bid Aveline a very pleasant night. Uncle Arnulf had disappeared into the library, feeling more like himself than he had in weeks. It was just the diversion Aveline needed.

Earlier in the evening, she had sent a note to Miss Leybourne asking for her assistance. The enthusiastic reply brought a smile to Aveline's face and warmed her heart. Both Leybourne sisters expressed their utter joy at Aveline's change of heart and were thrilled with the prospect of her becoming their sister-in-law. All that was left was to wait patiently for the appointed hour to arrive.

Time seemed to stand still. Aveline paced the length of her room waiting for nightfall. Several times doubt had crept into her mind. What if she got caught? What if he really didn't want her? What if...

When the clock struck ten, she gathered her things, peered out her door, and then snuck down the hall to the servant's stairwell, ignoring the protests in her stomach all the while. The house was quiet, and her flight went unseen. Aveline had never ventured out alone at night, or even during the day for that matter. It was quite the adventure.

Following the directions Miss Leybourne had given her, Aveline soon found herself at the servants' entrance to Leybourne House. A faint flame flickered in the window before the door opened slightly.

Miss Leybourne peered around the door. "This way, Miss Redgrave." Her soft voice urged Aveline into the house.

The butterflies in Aveline's stomach were fluttering about in ways that were alternately thrilling and frightening. She still could not believe she was sneaking into Leybourne House.

The single candle Miss Leybourne was holding illuminated their path, guiding them through the cold dark residence. Several minutes later they stopped at the threshold of a long hallway.

"Patrick retired a short time ago," Miss Leybourne whispered into Aveline's ear. "His door is the third on the left." It was almost impossible to hear the words over the rapid beating of her heart. Miss Leybourne raised a finger to her lips. "Shh."

Following close behind, Aveline was careful not to make a sound. When they reached Patrick's door, Miss Leybourne smiled brightly before scurrying down the hall, disappearing into the darkness.

Aveline contemplated her next course of action. Should she knock, or would the element of surprise be better? She stared at the door for countless seconds before saying a silent prayer. She lifted her hand, knocked softly then entered the chamber.

Patrick whipped around. The tenderness in his expression when their eyes met melted her heart. "Aveline." Her name rolled off his tongue like a melody. She had missed the deep sound of his voice caressing her soul. Any remaining apprehension vanished.

"May I come in?" She did not wait for his response, but closed the door and then brushed past him.

Forcing herself to remain calm, Aveline turned to face him. His dark brown eyes were wide with shock and confusion. He blinked several times as if he only imagined her presence. Patrick approached with caution, his eyes never leaving hers.

"What are you doing here?"

She pulled the paper that Patrick had given her uncle earlier in the day from her reticule. "I came to discuss the contents of the contract you presented to my uncle."

"At this hour?" His dark tired eyes showed the dullness of disbelief.

"Yes." She lifted her chin and uttered her rehearsed speech. "The terms are unacceptable."

Patrick glanced away for a moment, his expression turning somber. Aveline's heart pounded and her hands shook as she held the paper up and tore it in half. "I will not wait to be your wife." He stared, complete surprise on his face.

He closed the distance in two strides, and pulled her roughly into his embrace. She saw the fire and passion burn in his eyes moments before he took her mouth in an all-consuming kiss. His tongue explored with a hunger that matched her own. Patrick ran a firm hand down her back, possessively claiming her body.

With a growl, he swept her up into his arms. His eyes smoldered with a desire that sent shivers down her spine. "I want you." She had waited her whole life to hear those words. "Marry me." With those two simple words, he unlocked her heart and soul.

She drew his face to hers and kissed her reply across his lips, savoring the moment. Within seconds the kiss turned hungry as mutual desire consumed them. Without breaking the kiss, he carried her to the bed. With swift artful hands he slid her dress off her shoulders. Before she could gather her senses, he had stripped off her remaining clothes and was himself now lying naked beside her.

"I have dreamt of you like this since our first kiss."

Patrick explored her body, teasing, arousing. Her

skin tingled with the heat of his touch demanding more. Hot lips brushed across her nipple before his tongue caressed, then claimed the hardened bud. *Oh my*. Aveline thought she would die from pleasure. She arched her back, offering herself to his skilled mouth.

But it wasn't enough. Aveline wanted to explore his body and learn what excited him. She ran her hand across his broad chest reveling in the feel of his taut muscles. His sharp intake of breath as she brushed across his nipple delighted her. Feeling bolder, she lowered her head and explored his chest with her lips and tongue. His was an intoxicating scent that she could not quite place, but knew she wanted more of.

Patrick raised her chin, demanding her full attention. All she could think about was him, his body pressed so close to hers, and yet still so far away. She wriggled closer, desperate to feel more of his hard body.

Her hands caressed the strong planes of his back, moving upward and settling into his thick wavy hair. He gave a low growl before he moved his mouth over hers, smothering her lips with demanding mastery.

His hand gently massaged his way down her belly, and lower still. Shivers of delight followed his touch as he slid a hand between her thighs caressing the sensitive flesh with his fingers. A shudder of excitement jolted through her body.

"You are so wet for me," he whispered against her ear, before taking the lobe in a soft nibble.

"Is...is that a good thing?" The moment the words left her mouth, she mentally scolded herself for being so naïve.

Patrick's deep robust chuckle reverberated against her chest. "It is a very good thing, my love." He kissed the tip of her nose. "It means you're ready for me." He brushed a soft kiss on her cheek.

"I think I've been ready for you since the moment we first danced." Her body and soul craved his touch. They had the rest of their lives to go slow, to take their time. Aveline wanted to be his, and his alone. "I want you now."

The comment earned Aveline a seductive lopsided smile that made her pulse grow wild with anticipation of what was to come.

Moving his body to cover hers, he began to ease himself into her. "This may hurt."

Aveline could see the apprehension in his eyes and desperately wanted to reassure him. Through heavy breaths she said, "I trust you."

With one thrust, he broke through her barrier. Patrick took her mouth in a soft kiss, absorbing her cry. Her whole body tensed in response to the foreign invasion. He did not move for several seconds, giving her time to adjust.

He released her lips and whispered, "Just breathe and enjoy."

The pain was only momentary, quickly replaced by a simmering fire that demanded release. She took in a deep breath as he moved his hips, the full length of him enrapturing her core. Her body melted against his, becoming one. The kisses he showered along her neck sent a jolt of excitement through her body.

"You. Are. Mine." He breathed the possessive words across her slick skin. His expert touch sent her to even higher levels of pleasure.

Heat rippled through her as he guided her to a place too beautiful for words. "Oh Patrick," she cried out. Moments later she felt him shudder then relax against her.

Breathing heavily, he rolled onto his back, bringing her with him and held her snug within his embrace. Aveline rested her head against his wide chest. There was no place else she would rather be than here with him.

"I'm sorry I ever hurt you," he said with quiet emphasis. "I was desperate and..."

The restrained emotion in his voice brought tears to her eyes. She raised her head and pressed a finger to his lips. She did not want him to suffer anymore. "I know."

Patrick's hand cupped her cheek and held it gently. He gazed into her eyes with an intense honesty. "I'm in love with you. Never doubt that."

"I never will again." Aveline's heart overflowed with a joy she never thought possible. "I love you." For the first time in her life, she was blissfully happy, fully in love, and completely at peace.

Their lips met with a dreamy intimacy, carrying her away on a wispy cloud. He brushed soft seductive kisses along her cheek. The warmth of his kiss set her body aflame. She would never tire of his touch.

"Oh, Patrick, yes," she sighed as he kissed and nibbled his way down her neck.

He lifted his head, the teasing sparkle in his eyes smoldered with fire. "Does that mean you *will* marry me?"

She gazed into his loving brown eyes. Without any doubt or hesitation, she answered, "Yes, with all my heart, yes."

Epilogue

Seven months later

THE PAST SEVEN months with Aveline had been the happiest of Patrick's life. After they had married by special license, shocking the *ton* with their hasty nuptials, they retreated to the country to start building a new life together.

Within a matter of months, the estate had once again begun to prosper, far exceeding Patrick's expectations. Although Aveline insisted on using her dowry for repairs and renovations, Patrick was relieved the estate would soon be able to support itself. Aveline was more than a wife, she was a partner in all endeavors.

Patrick was able to put the past to rest and forgive his father. He'd severed all ties with Pickering and his prior life. There were more important things occupying his time. Everyday his love for his wife deepened and intensified.

"You look deep in thought." Aveline's silky voice

glided through the room.

"I was thinking about you," he said with all the love he felt in his heart.

Aveline strolled toward him. The seductive sway of her hips was a reminder of the pleasures they had shared only a couple of hours ago. She walked into his embrace and kissed him, pressing her lips to his, caressing his mouth.

"I am not going to finish any business if you keep kissing me like that," he teased.

Before she could respond, Dwight entered the room. "Pardon me, Lord Leybourne, the trunk has arrived. Shall I have it brought it in?"

"Yes, thank you." Patrick turned his attention back to Aveline, but she was too curious about the delivery.

"Trunk?" She raised a delicate brow in question. "Are we expecting your sisters?"

"No, they are still in London with Aunt Agnes and will meet us in Bath as scheduled."

"My aunt and uncle?"

"No, their plans have not changed either." Patrick was enjoying keeping Aveline in suspense.

She huffed out an inelegant sigh. "Well, then, what...?"

Patrick kissed the tip of her nose. "I am not going to reveal my surprise, you're just going to have to wait."

Moments later, two footmen brought in a large trunk and then retreated back to their posts.

"Open it," he encouraged her.

Brows creased together with uncertainty, she walked toward the trunk. He followed close behind, excited for her to see the contents.

She undid the latch and raised the lid. A white Holland cloth covered the hidden treasure. Patrick bent down, grabbed hold of the cloth and whisked it away from the trunk in one swoop.

"Oh...oh my," Aveline breathed out. "Patrick, it's the lion cub statue from Aunt and Uncle's London house. How...?" Her words trailed off as joyful tears streamed down her face.

"Shh, my love." Patrick enveloped her in his arms, and kissed the top of her head. "After you showed me your sketchbook, I wrote to your uncle inquiring after the statue. I offered a substantial sum for the little cub."

"Uncle Arnulf sold it to you?" Her words stuttered out, "It's one of his favorite...is...is he ill again?"

"Your uncle is still hale." Patrick felt the relief course through Aveline's body with his reassurance. "Actually, he refused my offer."

"But...why is it here?"

"Your aunt and uncle sent it to us as a belated

wedding present."

Even as the tears pooled in the corner of her eyes, Aveline's smile broadened. "Thank you," she whispered out.

Patrick cupped her face and wiped away the tears. "No, thank you. You saved me from a lifetime of sorrow and bitterness." He brushed a soft kiss across her smiling lips. "My life is complete with you by my side. I love you more than I ever thought possible."

"Oh, Patrick, you are my all, my one true love." Aveline reached up and sealed her declaration with a true love's kiss.

Chapter One Excerpt from:

Only a Hero Will Do

Alanna Lucas

Chapter One

ELIZABETH STROLLED INTO the stuffy, overly perfumed, and crowded ballroom. Some of the finest families of the *ton* were in attendance this evening. She pretended she had not a care in the world, but all the while took note of those around her.

Within the mass of well-dressed lords and ladies, Lord Fynes caught her eye, offering a slight nod toward the less crowded terrace. This was the signal she'd been waiting for all night.

Promenading the perimeter of the dance floor and heading toward the terrace, Elizabeth feigned interest in the quadrille, but continued to glance sideways at the portly Lord Baxter, the man she was to keep an eye on this evening.

Elizabeth had been given the tasks of attending social functions where Lord Baxter was present and taking note of whom he interacted with, and any other odd behavior. If it weren't for Lord Fynes' cryptic note about a stolen missive needing to be deciphered posthaste, and Lord Baxter's sudden decision to attend Lady Caper's ball this evening, she'd still be at home pretending to be ill. But these new developments took precedence over avoiding social obligations.

Elizabeth's mother, however, was thrilled with the last minute alteration to the evening's plans, promising Elizabeth would have a splendid time and declaring that, by the end of *this* season, her daughter was sure to have an offer of marriage. There was only one problem with her mother's theory; Elizabeth had no interest in marriage. Truth be told, she had never been a starry-eyed debutante setting her cap at handsome men. Not that she wasn't interested in the opposite sex. She just did not want to give up the life she'd worked so hard to build. She wanted to serve her country and help bring down Typhon, the Legion's mysterious and deadly enemy.

Despite the Legion's efforts to apprehend Typhon over the past several years, he'd continually managed to evade capture. After the last informant had turned up dead, all traces of Typhon and his miscreants had vanished, until last month when the Legion had received word from the Earl of Hartland stating he had uncovered information regarding influential members of the *ton* who were sympathetic to Typhon's anti-British cause. Lord Baxter's name was at the top of the list.

Lord Fynes' exuberant voice rose above the chatter, breaking into Elizabeth's reflections. "Miss Atwell, what an unexpected surprise it is to find you here this evening. I do hope your family is well. Is Lord Atwell in attendance?"

Elizabeth flicked her fan open. "My father is not in attendance, but is well, thank you, Lord Fynes." Glancing over her shoulder, she noticed Lord Baxter heading their way. The continual mopping of his brow, combined with his anxious expression and jittery movements, added to Elizabeth's suspicions. She didn't know if Lord Baxter suspected anything, but there was no time to contemplate the possibility. Lowering her voice, she spoke between waves of her fan. "What news?"

"Standard assignment to be delivered by Cap..." Lord Fynes halted his sentence before pasting a wide smile on his face, and in a boisterous voice exclaimed, "Lord Baxter! I was hoping we'd meet again this evening and continue our engaging discussion about the benefits of sea air on one's constitution."

Lord Baxter's face paled as little beads of sweat outlined the corners of his brow. "Oh yes, of course, sea air... one's constitution... perhaps later." He gulped the words down with force. Pulling out a white cloth from the edge of his coat, he wiped his brow with much force. "Quite warm this evening," was all the man could mutter before waddling away. It was difficult to believe the always-discomposed Lord Baxter could be involved in anything nefarious. Elizabeth suspected the man's immense wealth had attracted Typhon's attention.

Masking her thoughts, Elizabeth resumed the role of guest at Lady Caper's ball. "I had best be returning to my chaperone. It was a pleasure to see you this evening, Lord Fynes."

"Give your father my regards." Bowing slightly, Lord Fynes uttered under his breath, "Captain Alexander...tonight." Without further adieu, he took his leave, disappearing imperceptibly into the festive crowd.

Although she'd been deciphering messages for Lord Fynes since she was an adolescent, Elizabeth had only recently joined the ranks of the Legion, a secret organization created to destroy anything or anyone that might compromise the security of the realm. Thankfully her father had not objected, and her mother had no knowledge of her surreptitious activities.

The daughter of a viscount simply did not risk life and limb. No, the daughter of a viscount was expected to marry well, provide heirs, and know the latest *on dits*. The daughter of a viscount was expected to behave herself, do what she was told, and not be in possession of a weapon of any sort. Elizabeth had absolutely no interest in being that daughter.

She forced her best smile and prepared to wait. Patience was not her strong suit. Scanning the room, she looked for the man she'd heard so much about but had yet to meet. She'd been following his impressive military career for several years and was anxious to make his acquaintance.

When Typhon had struck again a few weeks past, Elizabeth was not surprised to learn Captain Alexander had been appointed to discover the identity of the man who had been slowly undermining British authority and weakening general confidence. Typhon's ultimate goal was to destroy the crown. His ever-expanding organization knew no boundaries, and it was the Legion's responsibility to bring him to justice. Elizabeth had no doubt Captain Alexander would be the man to accomplish such a feat, and she wanted nothing more than to be part of that team.

Anxious energy coursed through her limbs. If she stood still much longer, she might scream. Across the room, she spotted her chaperone, Lady Carteron—her recently married and dearest friend, Amelia— and decided to join her.

Elizabeth thought it quite ridiculous that, at the age of six and twenty, she still needed a chaperone. She did not quite understand how her younger friend provided any additional protection because of her recent change in marital status. Her mother and father, however, did not share her sentiment.

Girlish giggles followed by excited hushed whispers drifted over from a group of young ladies. The room quieted as all heads turned toward the entrance and the mysterious newcomer. It seemed as if every lady in attendance had noticed his arrival and were prepared to throw herself in his path.

He had the stature of a military man, proud and confident but not arrogant, and stood at least a head above most of the men in attendance. There was an air of danger and mystery about him that Elizabeth found intriguing. Could this be Captain Alexander?

Elizabeth strolled over to Amelia, but kept her eyes settled on the handsome gentleman in a dark blue coat. "Who is the impressively tall man?"

His gaze swept through the ballroom, resting on Elizabeth. Rapid flutters pattered against her chest as her eyes locked with the mysterious newcomer, catching her off guard. She quickly turned her gaze as if looking for someone.

Amelia leaned in and whispered, "That is Captain Grant Alexander. He's recently returned from Glanmire House."

Oh dear. Elizabeth had heard he was handsome, but he was a veritable Adonis!

"And standing next to him is Sir Simon," Amelia added.

Oh, so that is Sir Simon. Elizabeth had heard the numerous tales about his bravery, *and* his reputation with the ladies. She tried to suppress a giggle. Sir Simon's renown was second only to the Earl of Hartland's. She had no interest or time for rakes and scoundrels.

"They've been the best of friends since childhood."

Amelia always seemed to know everything about everyone. Calling her a gossip would have been a gross understatement. Except for the one not-so-minor flaw, Amelia would have made an excellent agent. However, she was instead a loyal friend who, without a doubt, would never betray Elizabeth's trust. Even still, Elizabeth had always acted with extreme caution regarding her other life. Few knew the truth of her association with the Legion, and she meant to keep it that way.

She happened another glance at Captain Alexander, who was now engaged in conversation with Lord Capers. His stoic features gave nothing away. She suspected that beneath the rigid and all too handsome façade was intelligence and compassion. There was just something about his aura that told her he was a good man. A good man and an excellent spy.

"What do you know of Captain Alexander?" Elizabeth questioned without thought, wanting to know more than just of his military career. Not that she had any interest in the Captain beyond the professional, but she'd often found a person's past influenced their present course.

Take herself, for example. Elizabeth had always been told she would never be able to fire a pistol, or hit a target with an arrow, or have a place in a man's world. But the moment her late grandfather had revealed his secret, she'd instantly known the path her life would take. She was going to prove every naysayer wrong.

Amelia took in a deep breath and began to rattle off the facts. "He was a sickly child, often bedridden. Both his parents died when he was still fairly young and has no other living relatives. He has served in the military, but no one knows much about his service apart from his strong sense of honor and duty. He has traveled extensively and speaks multiple languages. Rumor has it that his late grandfather had amassed quite a fortune in trade and acquired Brookhurst, a lovely property near the Peak District. He's not married." Elizabeth eyed her friend, about to ask if that was all the information Amelia had on Captain Alexander when she added, "Oh, and he's thirty years old and has managed to keep all romantic entanglements out of the gossips' ears. Other than that, his life is shrouded in mystery."

"Yes, shrouded in mystery." Somehow Elizabeth was able to hold in the laughter. Apart from extremely personal details, Amelia had covered all the basics.

How would she approach him without raising suspicion? Did Captain Alexander know who she was? Perhaps he already applied to the master of ceremonies for an introduction.

Elizabeth contemplated her next course of action when Mr. Cokinbred, one of many fortune hunters in attendance, sauntered to where she and Amelia were standing.

"Lady Carteron," Mr. Cokinbred said in a polite, if not slightly condescending tone, before turning his attention to Elizabeth. "Miss Atwell, it is a pleasure to see you this evening." His smile widened revealing a set of ill-maintained teeth. "May I have the pleasure of the next dance?"

Propriety dictated she accept, but conformity was not a common word in Elizabeth's vocabulary. "I thank you for the offer, but I am rather tired at present."

Mr. Cokinbred's face turned to an unflattering shade of red. Under his breath he muttered, "Good evening," before storming away, clearly displeased with Elizabeth's refusal.

Amelia leaned in and, with a teasing whisper, said, "Your mother will be none too pleased when she hears of your refusal to dance."

Ignoring Amelia's comment, Elizabeth shifted her attention back to the dance floor. The orchestra was in place and guests were lining up for the next set. Sir Simon had already secured his dance partner. She noticed Captain Alexander standing alone off to one side, surveying his surroundings. Despite the lack of gentlemen in attendance, he had yet to ask a lady to dance. Perhaps he was not as much of a gentleman as she'd first thought him to be.

A group of colorful young debutantes paraded in front of Elizabeth, obstructing her view of Captain Alexander. How was she to catch his eye if she couldn't even see him? By the time the young ladies flitted past, he was nowhere to be seen.

She flicked open her fan for the second time in a span of fifteen minutes and began fanning herself fervently. It was becoming quite the undesirable habit.

"Are you alright, Elizabeth dear?"

Elizabeth clutched her chest with her other hand and let out a long sigh. "It is rather warm this evening. I fear I may be taking ill."

Amelia raised a single delicate brow, her eyes narrowing with a dubious look. They'd been friends a long time and Amelia instantly knew when Elizabeth was up to something. "I find it rather pleasant this evening," she teased.

Keeping with her charade for those who might overhear, Elizabeth continued to fan herself. "I believe I just need a moment's reprieve. Do you happen to know the way to the ladies' retiring room?"

"Down the hall." Amelia pointed before adding in a hushed tone, "The same direction in which Captain Alexander disappeared a short time ago."

Elizabeth snapped her fan closed. "I don't know why I even bother."

"Because I am your dearest friend and want to help." Although Amelia did not know the specifics of Elizabeth's involvement, she had always suspected it had something to do with the government. On numerous occasions she had tried to weasel it out of Elizabeth, all in good fun of course, but Elizabeth had never conceded. Amelia had promised on pain of torture and death never to reveal what she suspected. And she had never given Elizabeth cause to doubt that promise.

Elizabeth smiled. "Thank you. I won't be long."

Edging along the perimeter of the crowd, Elizabeth trudged toward the ladies' retiring room under the charade of illness. Upon reaching the hall, she resumed her normal pace. Except for several elegantly dressed ladies parading back toward the ballroom, ready to resume their husband-hunting antics, the hall was empty.

Where did he disappear?

Just then, a slight shadow near a fluted column caught her attention. Even before she saw him, she felt his larger than life presence. *Captain Alexander.*

Strolling around the column, she pretended to admire a rather grotesque orange, green, and gold floral vase. Captain Alexander was leaning against the wall, partially hidden from view by another column and a decorative pedestal. Her earlier assessment of him did not do him justice. He *was* like a Greek god, but more handsome and far less arrogant.

"Have you noticed that Mr. Devlin's bays are mismatched?" His soft deep voice sent a tingle all the way down to her toes, catching her off guard for a moment.

What was wrong with her? Despite the many attempts by the *ton's* most handsome rakes and scoundrels, she'd never been this distracted by anyone before.

Breathing in deeply to steady her nerves, she swallowed the hard lump in her throat. Neither attempt was of any use. Ignoring the intense fluttering in her heart, she replied in code, "Yes, I believe he acquired them in Dublin."

Captain Alexander surveyed both directions before nodding toward a partially opened door. Elizabeth glanced behind to ensure no one was watching and then followed him into the dark drawing room.

It took a moment for her eyes to adjust to her surroundings. Slowly, a couple of sofas flanking a large table came into focus.

Captain Alexander came up beside her, turned and faced the door. The aroma of fresh soap and leather encircled Elizabeth, infiltrating her senses. They were common enough scents, but on him were intoxicating and far too intriguing.

"It's a pleasure to finally meet you, Miss Atwell." His words were a mere whisper. "And quite an honor that you side-stepped Mr. Cokinbred *and* left your chaperone to meet with me." The teasing tone in his voice made her insides tingle. For the first time in her life she understood why her sisters all swooned at the sight of a handsome man.

"I do not care for the rules of the *ton*, especially when they are far inferior to protecting and safeguarding our country. I believe you share this sentiment, Captain Alexander?"

A slight laugh escaped his lips. "Yes, I would assume Lady Carteron informed you of who I was and told you my entire life story?"

"Only the highlights." Elizabeth confessed with a nervous giggle. *Focus on the task at hand.* "I understand you have something for me?"

Captain Alexander took her gloved hand and slipped a folded piece of paper into her palm, then closed her fingers over the small missive. The motion seemed intimate, inappropriate, and all too enticing. A strange inner excitement coursed through her veins.

"Guard this well. Lord Fynes will be calling on your father first thing in the morning."

Captain Alexander did not wait for her response, but disappeared further into the darkness of the drawing room. A cool breeze and another hint of fresh soap and leather drifted through the space, followed by the soft *click* of a door closing.

Elizabeth took the folded letter and smoothed it across her chest, tucking it into her dress and nestling it on the outer curve of her breast. The intense beating of her heart was a steady staccato against her hand. She sighed deeply, letting her head fall back against the wall.

"Elizabeth," a soft voice questioned from the hall.

At least she wouldn't have to pretend to be flustered. Captain Alexander had aided her sufficiently with that unwanted response.

She edged off the wall, smoothed her hand across her chest, ensuring the missive was securely hidden, and then strolled toward the doorway. "In here, Amelia."

Before Elizabeth reached the door, Amelia pushed it open, allowing candlelight from the hall to filter into the drawing room, casting eerie distorted shadows across the walls. "What are you doing in here?" She glanced about as if expecting to find someone.

"I just needed a quiet moment." After her brief encounter with Captain Alexander, that was the truth.

"You are missing all the dancing. I promised Lady Atwell I would not let you be a wallflower this evening. You already turned away Mr. Cokinbred. If you don't make an effort, your mother will not ask me to chaperone again, and then where will you be?"

Elizabeth had never been a wallflower in her entire life. Her decision not to be social had nothing to do with shyness, but an intense unwillingness to abide by the *ton's* rules. But Amelia was right. She had to make an effort, or else risk having her mother at her side at each and every future event of the season until she was married off. A fierce shudder replaced the delightful tingling she'd felt only a moment ago.

She sucked in her breath and forced her best I'm-enjoying-the-evening smile. She might look the part of a viscount's daughter, but inside beat the heart of a spy.

Grant was relieved to be back in the quiet of his room. He found social functions more draining than marching in the rain through ankle-deep mud. Sighing deeply, he enjoyed the silence that afforded him time alone with his thoughts. The evening had not turned out as expected.

When he'd informed Lord Fynes about the missive he'd recovered and whom he believed had written it, he'd expected his superior to handle it himself. But when Grant received orders that he was to deliver the coded missive to Miss Atwell, he'd expected an old spinster who dabbled in amateur mysteries. However, instead of an elderly woman on the cusp of death, a lady who could bring any man in a room to his knees had greeted him. Not just greeted him, but enticed him in a way no other female had before.

Sinking into the warm comfort of the leather chair, Grant's thoughts strayed to Miss Atwell. She had turned down a dance and left her chaperone's side, all to accept a missive? Her large brown eyes held an intelligence far beyond her youthful years, and then there was her luxurious brown hair that glistened beneath the candlelight, not to mention her voice...her voice was pure heaven. She was the type of woman dreams were made of— entirely perfect, but far out of Grant's reach. Miss Atwell was the daughter of a viscount, lest he forget that not so minor detail.

How was it even possible the daughter of a viscount was the Legion's top decoder? And why hadn't he known about her previously?

From Lord Fynes he had learned she was able to decipher codes faster than any man, and also had a knack for puzzles. It was a talent that made her highly valuable to the organization in this game where time was of the essence.

When he'd pressed Lord Fynes for further details about Miss Atwell's background and qualifications, he'd been warned that the information was classified. Although Grant understood the need for discretion, he detested all the secrecy. It made it difficult for him to do his job and protect his team when he didn't have all the facts.

He swirled the brandy in his glass, watching the liquid slowly ripple to a gentle stop. Lifting the glass to his lips, he inhaled the fragrant aroma before taking a long, slow sip. The fiery liquid burned as it traveled down his throat and settled into his gut. Why would a lady born to privilege want to do such work?

Grant suspected he could drink all night and still not be rid of the image of the beautiful and intelligent Miss Atwell. He was far too intrigued by her, and not just in the physical sense.

About the Author

Multi-published historical romance author Alanna Lucas grew up in Southern California, but always dreamed of distant lands and bygone eras. From an early age, she took an interest in history and travel, and is thrilled to incorporate those diversions into her writing. Alanna writes Regency-set historical romance.

When she is not daydreaming of her next travel destination Alanna can be found researching, spending time with family, or going for long walks. She makes her home in California with her husband, children, one sweet dog, and hundreds of books.

Just for the record, you can never have too many shoes, handbags, or books. And travel is a must.

If you'd like to find out more about Alanna or her books you can visit her website: www.alannalucas.com

Other Books by Alanna Lucas

Only a Hero Will Do

Defender of the realm...and his wary heart...

Captain Grant Alexander is an enigma in London society. Dashing and handsome, he coldly eschews marriage. But the ton knows nothing of his role in the Legion: to bring Typhon, the traitor who seeks to destroy the British monarchy, to justice.

When Grant is thrown together with fellow Legion member Elizabeth Atwell, he's instantly beguiled yet exasperated by this beautiful viscount's daughter. She has little interest in combing the marriage mart for a well-bred, well-heeled husband, but is adept at code-breaking and handling a bow and arrow. She also refuses to do as she is told, insisting she accompany Grant on his mission.

As Typhon continues to evade capture and dark forces are at work, Grant realizes he must act, not only to protect the realm but Elizabeth too...not to mention his heart, which is in danger of thawing every time she comes close...

In His Arms Series

Face to Face
When We Dance
Mistletoe Waltz
Dancing Around the Truth
Wish Upon a Waltz
Dancing with the Earl

~ ~ ~

A Marchioness for Christmas
Three Yuletide Wishes

~ ~ ~

Only a Hero Will Do

Historical Westerns

Once Upon a Montana Christmas
A Cowboy's Mistletoe Promise

Coming Soon...

When the Marquess Returns